Copyright © 2020 Olivia Hayle

All rights reserved. No part of this publication may be distributed or transmitted without the prior consent of the publisher, except in case of brief quotations embodied in articles or reviews.

All characters and events depicted in this book are entirely fictitious. Any similarity to actual events or persons, living or dead, is purely coincidental.

The following story contains mature themes, strong language and explicit scenes, and is intended for mature readers.

Cover by by Sarah Armitage Design
Edited by Stephanie Parent
www.oliviahayle.com

BILLION DOLLAR BEAST

When you are afraid, all love disappears.
When you love a person, all fears disappear.

- Osho

1

BLAIR

I'm at a wedding out of state when I'm confronted with my worst enemy. I spot him before he spots me: across the crowded reception hall, wearing a suit disdainfully, like he wants to shrug it off and transform into the brute he is inside.

Enemy might be too tame a word. *Nightmare* is a much better description. For a people-pleaser like me, he's a personal affront. I've tried to make him my friend for near on a decade and I've failed for just as long.

He takes a sip of his brandy and sweeps a dark gaze over the guests. I'll be noticed any second now. How had I not known he'd been invited to this wedding?

"Is that Nicholas Park?" Maddie asks at my side, speaking his name with obvious relish. I wish I could say no. I want to tell her that his reputation isn't deserved, that he's not that special when you've seen him drunk and disheveled.

But that would be lying.

"Yes," I say, feeling like I'm confirming something far more than just his name. Because even drunk and disheveled, he's absolutely magnificent.

"Aren't you two friends?"

"He's my *brother's* friend."

Maddie's laughter is a bit too high-pitched. "Well, that's even better! You have to introduce me, Blair."

"I don't think so."

"Why not?" Her voice drops. "Is what they say of him true, then? Is it better to stay away?"

"I wouldn't know," I say, though I do. It's definitely better to stay away. I've been trying to for the better part of a decade, but like a bad rash, he keeps returning, and there are no over-the-counter remedies in sight.

"I've heard that he once burned down a club he owned, just to get the insurance money." Maddie's voice is vibrating with delight at the idea of Nick committing fraud. "I had no idea he'd be here today. Did you know he was invited?"

"No," I say honestly. "I had absolutely no idea. I can't imagine he knows either the bride *or* the groom."

I reach up to run a hand through my hair and glance casually around the room. Nick is leisurely strolling through the throng of people with his glass in hand. Despite his suit, he looks out of place amongst the mingling guests in brightly colored dresses and dark tuxes—like a fox in a hen house. Who'd left the gate unlocked?

"Introduce me, Blair," Maddie urges again. "Come on."

And before I can protest, her hand is on my arm and I'm pulled forward on my heels. They dip into the grass with every step I take.

Nick sees us approach, his eyes flitting past Maddie to bore into mine.

Dark, so dark, and not a hint of amusement in them. His lips grow thinner, the rough cut of his jawline working once. So he hadn't expected to see me here, either.

"Blair," he says. The gravel in his voice is no surprise to me, but it still makes my stomach tight with nerves.

"Nick."

Beside me, Maddie preens. I clear my throat. "This is Madeleine Bishop. She's a friend from college. We both know the bride."

She extends her hand and Nick gives it a brief shake, face impassive.

"A pleasure," she says smoothly. It's her flirting voice—I recognize it from our partying days.

Nick doesn't acknowledge it. He nods to the bar behind us instead. "The groom was on the thirty under thirty list in *Forbes*, but can't shell for an open bar?"

Maddie laughs, like he's being unbelievably clever. I cross my arms over my chest. "So you know the groom?"

"That's not what I said."

"So you're here on the bride's invitation?"

His eyes flit back to mine. "Wouldn't you like to know?" he asks. "But I think I'll keep you guessing. Ladies, it's been a pleasure."

And then he strides off toward the bar without a second glance. Beside me, Maddie turns to me with incredulous eyes. "*Wow,*" she breathes. "You weren't kidding. You two really aren't friends."

"That's what I said," I say tersely, running a hand over my hair again. It shouldn't be a sore subject. It's been years, after all, since my big brother befriended Nicholas Park. And still, his dislike of me stings like salt in a never-closing wound.

Maddie takes the hint. "Let's ignore him altogether," she says. "They're dividing guests into teams. Come on, let's join."

I take another sip of my champagne and give her a bright smile. We're at a wedding. We're here to celebrate love and life and happiness. The sun is shining. It shouldn't be difficult to put Nicholas Park out of my mind.

"Let's," I say.

But as it turns out, that's absolutely *impossible* to do when he refuses to stay out of sight. I'm standing in line for the cornhole toss when a shadow stalks in beside me. Like an electric current sliding over my skin, I know who it is before he speaks.

"Blair Porter, Seattle's top socialite, playing outdoor games."

I roll my neck and pretend to ignore the jab. I fail. "It's a time-

3

honored sport. Besides, as a guest of the wedding party, you're supposed to attend all the wedding festivities."

"And I suppose you think I haven't?"

I squeeze my lips tight to prevent my words from spilling out. I manage restraint for a proud five seconds. "I hadn't seen you at any of the pre-ceremony events."

"Well, I've never been good at following rules."

"Why were you invited, anyway? Who do you really know here?"

He raises a dark eyebrow. "Such skepticism, Blair. Don't you think I have friends?" The mocking tone in his voice makes it clear that the question is rhetorical. I answer it regardless.

"Other than my brother? No."

He steps up beside me. Somewhere from the corner of my eye, I see Maddie slink back in line, abandoning me to my new partner. Damn.

Nick doesn't answer my question. "This is a wedding to be seen at," he says smoothly. "Have you seen how many photographers they've hired? Why do you think *you* were invited?"

My stomach churns at the question. Becca and I had been friends in college… Sure, we hadn't spoken much since, but I hadn't thought twice about accepting the invitation to her wedding.

"You're saying I'm a trophy guest." I speak the words harshly, like they don't offend me.

Nick raises an eyebrow. The sharp sunlight throws his rough features into relief. "Tell me Cole wasn't invited as well."

Bending down to pick up a corn-bag, I weigh it in my hand, refusing to answer his taunt.

Nick's voice is satisfied. "He was, then. But he didn't come."

"He couldn't," I say, hating how defensive the words sound. At the time, it didn't seem odd that Becca had invited my billionaire big brother. I'd thought it a kindness. How had I been so stupid?

If Nick sees my realization, he doesn't acknowledge it. He unbuttons the clasp of his gray suit jacket instead, a smirk on his lips. He must be aware of the way the other guests are watching him. Watching us.

"Is that why you were invited too? For the press and prestige?"

Nick's chuckle isn't amused. He understands the words as I'd meant them—having him attend an event made it noteworthy, but not always in a particularly good way. If my brother is seen as a powerful businessman, Nick is the unscrupulous one.

"We're up," he says instead, voice like crushed glass. "Don't miss."

And of course I do. Despite my aim, there's no scoring after his words. The opposing teams cheers, high-fiving each other.

When I turn to Nick, his lip is curled. "I told you not to."

"I didn't know I needed advice."

"It couldn't hurt."

I grit my teeth against the annoyance that rises up inside me. I'm a happy person. I like to smile and converse and make people happy. It's what I'm good at, damn it. And somehow Nicholas Park *always* makes me forget that.

No longer. I give him a blinding smile. Judging by the faint widening of his eyes, it wasn't what he'd been expecting.

"Here, why don't *you* throw the next one."

He accepts the corn-bag I hand him with suspicious eyes. "I see," he says. And that's all he says, even as he lines himself up, focusing on the cornhole. Tall and muscular, with wide shoulders, he's an imposing figure. Always has been.

He throws. It flies in an arc through the air and lands solidly in the hole. I don't look him in the eyes—I turn away instead, but I don't head to the back of the line.

Nick follows me towards the bar.

"What are you doing?"

"I'm participating in the wedding activities. I was recently told that I wasn't being a good guest."

"Why are you really here?"

His gaze fastens on something in the distance. I'm left staring

5

up at the column of his throat, the rough-hewn features that have held me captive for ages.

"Nick, I—"

"Shh."

"Did you just shush me?"

He looks down at me, speculation in his gaze. His words come quickly. "Pretend you like me for fifteen minutes."

I blink at him. "Fifteen minutes?"

"I know it's a rather long time frame," he grinds out, "but yes, fifteen minutes."

"No one's that good an actress," I mutter. He rolls his eyes at my words.

And then Nick does the most amazing thing. He puts a hand on my low back, like it belongs there, as if he touches me all the time—as if this isn't the first time we've touched since we shook hands eight years ago.

He bends down. "Look up at me," he instructs. "Laugh as if you enjoy talking to me."

"Why?" I hiss back.

Brief hesitation. "I'll owe you one."

"Whatever I want?"

Longer hesitation this time. "Within reason, yes."

I turn on my biggest smile, then. The one that stretches wide and reaches my eyes. It's my killer mingling smile, the one I only pull out when I really need to pack a punch. "Fifteen minutes," I say, batting my eyelashes. "Start the timer."

Nick blinks once. Twice. Then he gives a subtle nod to a few men standing not too far from us, drinks in hand.

"See the one with glasses?"

"Yes."

His hand drifts higher, flattening against my back. The touch is warm even through the fabric of my dress. "I'm going to talk to him, and I want you by my side as I do."

"Pretending to like you."

"Yes."

"Why?"

"Need to know basis, honey," he says sweetly. The endearment sounds mocking from him.

"All right, sugar muffin," I respond just as tartly. "Fourteen minutes left."

He grits his teeth audibly at that.

The men look up as we approach, their conversation abruptly dying.

"Mr. Park," the man in glasses says. His tone is cold. "I didn't know you'd be here."

"Last-minute invite," Nick says, an odd tone in his voice. Is that… gentleness? He must be trying to win points here somehow. "This is Blair Porter."

I extend a hand, still smiling widely. "A pleasure to meet you all."

They introduce themselves. "I've met your brother a few times," the man in glasses—Mr. Adams—says. "Lovely guy."

I resist the urge to glance at Nick. So that's why I'm here, smiling at him. He's using me in all of my trophy invitedness. "Yes, he is," I say, leaning into Nick's side. "Despite being friends with this one."

They laugh at my joke and Nick is forced to join in. The pressure of his hand on my back increases in a not so subtle warning to behave. *Idiot,* I think. *I just made you look more likeable.*

"That's right," Nick says. "We've known each other for what, eight years now, Blair?"

"Something like that," I say.

The shorter of the three men smiles at me. "I hope you'll stay long enough to meet my wife. She's around here somewhere, and she reads every style interview you give."

"That's lovely," I say warmly. "I'd love to meet her."

Nick clears his throat and I tear my gaze away to look up at him expectantly, forcing friendliness into my gaze.

"Enjoying the time away from Seattle?" Nick's question is open-ended, but his entire body language is focused on Mr. Adams. *Subtle,* I think, wondering how Nick would react to my hand on his back in warning.

7

"I am, yes," Mr. Adams says. "Some time away can be good. Clears the head."

Nick nods gravely. "Lends itself to making excellent decisions."

"This is not the place to discuss business," Mr. Adams retorts. The two men at his side both look away, clearly uncomfortable with the turn of conversation. Nick is tense beside me.

This won't do.

I put a hand on his arm affectionately, looking over at Mr. Adams with a smile. "Even at a wedding," I say, making my voice light. "Can you believe it? It's impossible to get this guy to relax!"

Nick sighs. "About as impossible as you walking past a store without purchasing anything."

"Well, we all have our vices," I tease, my wide smile still in place. "I'm sorry we bothered you."

"Not at all," Mr. Adams says. "It was a pleasure to meet you, Miss Porter."

"Likewise."

The three men stroll on, leaving Nick and I to revel in our peaceful, friendly bliss. I hit his arm.

"What the hell was that for?"

"You call me a trophy guest, someone invited here for appearance's sake, and then you use me in just the same way?"

There's no remorse or denial in Nick's eyes. Just sly calculation. "You did well."

"I was coerced."

"No, you weren't. Now I owe you one." He speaks the words with obvious distaste.

I put my hands on my hips. "So you're what? Trying to take over his company? Buy out his board? Tank his stocks?"

Nick narrows his eyes at me. "You don't need to know," he says, articulating every word.

I flick my hair over my shoulder and feel a faint sense of triumph as his eyes track the movement. "Well, that was the first and last time you use my name to boost your reputation."

8

"Trust me, it's *definitely* the last time." He takes a sip of his drink and mutters something that sounds an awful lot like *not worth it*.

I shake my head at him and start to head back to the festivities, to people who actually enjoy having me around.

"Running back to your sycophant friends?" he throws after me.

"Don't you have a hostile takeover to plan?"

His crooked grin is wolfish. "Good idea," he says. "I heard a few of the bridesmaids are single…"

"Oh, screw you."

"Are you offering? I don't think your fifteen minutes are entirely up yet."

"You wish," I hiss, retreating across the lawn before he has a chance to answer. How much easier my life would be if my brother hadn't decided to become best friends with the least friendly man on the planet. Infuriating, maddening, and absolutely impossible to ignore.

I remember the first time I'd seen him. It had been nearly a decade ago, when he'd stalked into the restaurant together with my brother for dinner. I'd had no advance warning that my brother's friend would be joining us. That was Cole's way, sometimes, especially in those days—he did what pleased him, like a bulldozer or a rocket. You could either stand in his way and get crushed, or adapt to his speed. Over the years, I've gotten very good at adapting.

Nick had worn their college jersey, ironically, like it was beneath him. I'd never seen a man who moved like he did—he walked like a street fighter.

He'd joined our table with a perfunctory nod to me.

"This is Nicholas Park," my brother had said, flipping open the menu. "We're seniors together."

"A pleasure to meet you," I said, extending a hand. He'd

looked at it once before he shook it. I remember that clearly—his brief hesitation.

That's when I'd felt the scars on the inside of his palm. Faint, but raised, and unmistakable. The surprise in my gaze must have been easy for him to read. He'd withdrawn his hand and opened his menu.

And that had been that. I'd been too intimidated—too impressed, to be honest—to speak much during that dinner. The next time Cole and I were alone, I'd peppered him with questions about Nick. I'd done it with an air of impetuousness, and he'd rolled his eyes at his annoying little sister and all her questions. He'd never realized that my inquiries came from a place of burning curiosity and genuine interest.

Because handsome was far too tame a word for Nicholas Park. There was a slight crook to his nose that gave his face character; his black hair was cut too short to be fashionable. And yet, the olive tone to his skin, the dark of his eyes, the wildness in his jaw…

I'd been struck.

And then he'd struck me.

Oh, not like that, of course. But his verbal spear had found its mark just the same. That damn party and that damn poker game. Even recalling it eight years later, it makes my cheeks burn with indignity. Anger. The way he'd turned me down with a tone of voice that was so cold it burned.

He'd been playing poker. The room was smoke-filled, the air heady, the tension around the table high. I'd walked straight in. It had been foolish—I can admit that much in retrospect. I barely knew anyone at the table; Walker was the older brother of one of my childhood friends, and our fathers worked together. But the rest were strangers.

Apart from Nick.

He'd seen me when I'd walked in. His eyes had met mine for a few seconds and then he'd refocused on his cards like I was nothing at all. There hadn't even been a hint of recognition in his eyes.

That should have been a sign, really. But I'd had two and a half glasses of wine and I was heady with nerves and excitement. Nick was here at this party, without my brother in tow. We'd already been introduced. I was his best friend's little sister.

It was time he saw me as something other than that.

So I planned on joining the game with a couple of hundred bucks to my name. It was a lot, and I was reluctant to risk it, but my reluctance was worn thin by the memory of Nick's sharp-edged jaw.

I was brave-verging-on-stupid.

I stopped next to Nick, almost leaning on his chair. He didn't acknowledge me.

"Good game?" I asked.

"Can't tell until it's over," he'd responded. A few of the guys around the table had smiled at that, like the answer was obvious, like I'd been a fool for asking.

That didn't dissuade twenty-one-year-old me. "Deal me in? I have the cash."

At that, Nick had actually put down his cards. The other guys were looking at me then. Some with interest in their eyes—one of them ran his gaze up my form in a way that was nothing short of lewd.

Nick met my gaze. The eyes gave me no quarter, offered no mercy. They were dark like coal and just as fiery.

"This isn't a game for little girls," he said. "Run back to your friends now."

Maybe it would have been okay if he'd said it as a joke. If there had been a teasing note to his voice, a bit of irony. Perhaps even anger—I'd know what to do with that. But the cold civility in his tone shocked me to my core. It was a dismissal. I wasn't used to being dismissed.

That was the first time I'd reached out to Nick in the hopes of being friends, and it was the first time he rejected me out of hand.

But it wouldn't be the last.

2

NICK

"Thank you, gentlemen," I say, shaking their hands in turn, my grip firm. Three generations of Adams's look back at me with varying levels of hostility. I don't add any more words. I don't tell them that this was an affair well-done or that they'll be pleased. I'm fairly certain they won't be by the time my ownership of the company is finished.

Old Mr. Adams gives me a nod. "You take care of our business now, young man."

I want to grit my teeth at the epitaph, but nod. If by taking care you mean tearing it apart and selling the pieces to the highest bidder, then yes. Sure.

They filter out of my office, having just agreed to sell their family business and life's work. Gina is waiting by the door with a practiced smile. She'll escort them out and go over the final paperwork, far away from the man who essentially gave them no choice in the matter.

Me.

Leaning back in the chair, I put my hands at my temples. Victory. This is victory, and it still doesn't taste sweet enough.

It had become a drug, this. Playing the long game. Taking over companies. Buying them for a pittance.

Selling them for parts.

I flip my pen over in my grip and pull up the company's website again. B.C. Adams. An old, respectable clothing chain, as all-American as apple pie and stuffed turkey and checkered picnic tablecloths. Just sold to me by one Pierce Adams, Pierce Adams Jr., and Bryce Adams.

This deal had been months in the making. My company had circled them since last year's quarter reports left investors reeling. The company was floundering. At its current state, it's only a matter of months before bankruptcy is a given.

One after one, other potential buyers were scared off by the abysmal financial results. One I had taken care of myself by spreading a false rumor about an upcoming merger and acquisition. They'd dropped out of the race right before I'd swooped in with my final offer.

The board had been all for accepting. Like rats deserting a sinking ship, they saw me for the piece of flotsam I was.

The three Adams's? Not so much.

That's why I'd gone to that godforsaken wedding in Oregon in the first place. Pierce Adams Jr. would be there, attending as a friend of the groom, so I needed to be there too. Show that I was a man to be trusted. That I could kiss babies and hug women. *Could you grab a beer with him?*

I wasn't running for president, but it felt damn near close when I needed to have all three of the Adams's votes. Using Blair Porter's heavenly smile to help with that had been a stroke of brilliance.

Just the memory of her conjures up familiar feelings of frustration and anger. Blonde hair the color of wheat, curling around a heart-shaped face. Honey-brown eyes that I most often saw narrowed in annoyance.

She'd been angry to see me, a spitting kitten with her hackles raised. That was true to form. For as long as I'd known her, she'd been angry with me for one reason or another. Good.

Anger I could handle—anger I liked.

And the scolding she'd given me at the end… *I can't believe you used me for your business deal!*

It almost brought a smile to my face, just remembering it. Basking in her anger felt a bit like basking in the sunlight. Both equally fiery and all-consuming.

And then she'd been gone in a flurry of silky fabric and flowing hair, back to her harem of low-tier socialites and fans.

I shake my head at my own thoughts. Blair Porter has already occupied too much of my time today. It's time to focus on the far easier task at hand—and that's turning a failing clothing giant around enough so that I can butcher it profitably.

When I arrive at one of Cole's properties in the evening, he's already waiting for me by the tennis courts. In his white shorts and T-shirt, he looks pristine, every inch the golden-boy billionaire he is. He hates it when I call him a blue blood, but that's exactly what he looks like. The Porters were rich long before he began building his empire.

"Hey," he says, lobbying a tennis ball hard at my chest. I catch it before it makes contact. "I heard you ran into Blair at the wedding last weekend."

Had she tattled to her brother? A pang of disappointment hits me. She usually kept our banter private.

"I did."

I take my place at the baseline and Cole is forced to raise his voice. "And you both made it out alive?"

"Evidently." I call back, tossing the ball high and serving, ignoring the fact that he's not in the right spot. He handles it deftly and for the coming minutes there's nothing but the sound of tennis balls against racquets and the thrill of the game. I lose myself in the fight, as I so often did when I was young, surrendering to the pumping of blood and adrenaline.

Cole might come from different stock—he has a background of athletic competitions and trophies—but the thrill of the hunt is the same.

We're well-matched, have been after playing so many times

together over the years. By the time we're done, we're panting, chugging from our water bottles.

"Damn," he says finally. "Have you been practicing with an Olympian while I was away? Your slices are deadly."

I grin at him. "I had a good morning."

He braces himself against the edge of the net. Sweat glistens on his skin; I'm sure I look much the same. "Did you close the deal, then?"

"I just did, yeah."

His face lights up into a smile, and for a moment it's uncomfortably similar to Blair's—not that she's ever smiled at *me* like that. "Hell yes. Well done, man!"

"Took me long enough."

"Can you finally tell me which company it is? I need to know where to shop one last time."

"B.C. Adams."

His smile fades. "Shit. Really?"

"Yeah."

"That chain is massive. And failing. People have been placing bets on how long it'll stay afloat."

"Well, a little bit longer at least. I need to squeeze out a profit from it first."

Cole runs a hand through his hair. "Fuck," he says again. "A clothing chain. They must have massive stores of inventory."

"I'm betting on that, yeah."

"And you need to flip it fast to pay the overhead. Do you know anything about retail?"

Uncomfortable though it is to admit, I answer him truthfully. "No. But I'll hire people who do."

He bends down to tie his shoelaces. The wedding band on his left hand shines golden in the sunlight. The man had become near insufferable with happiness after his wedding to Skye. "Hire Blair," he suggests. "She knows fashion."

I stare down at him. "What?"

"She studied business and fashion. She had that fashion brand a few years back, remember?"

15

Yes, I do, and the memory isn't a good one. She'd launched a collection at twenty-three that had crashed and burned not two years later. Not exactly a ringing endorsement.

But even if that wasn't the case—even if she was the most qualified person on the planet—there's no way she'd work with me.

"I remember," I say. "But…"

"But what?" Cole meets my gaze baldly. I know he won't accept a bad word about Blair. I'm on thin ice, and for the first time in a long while, I can feel the danger. Cole gives me a lot of leeway, sure, but absolutely none when it comes to his family.

But then it hits me.

There's no way she'd agree.

"It's a good idea," I say. "You're right, she knows the industry. I could hire her as a consultant."

Cole's shoulders relax. "It would be good for her. For you both, I'm sure. Who knows, maybe you can both finally learn how to get along?"

I nod, though my agreement is an absolute lie.

It sounds like a nightmare.

"I'll ask her," Cole continues. "I'm seeing her later."

"Good." I swing my bag up on my shoulder and make my face impassive. She's going to say no—what excuse she'll use to Cole, I don't know. But if there's one thing I'm sure of, it's that Blair Porter has never hated anyone more than she hates me.

3

BLAIR

"Do you never lock the front door?"

"Not when you have a front gate." My brother leans against the kitchen island, still in his dirty gym clothes, a protein shake in hand.

"Have you abandoned showering?"

He shoots me a *don't-start* look. "I just got back from playing with Nick."

I ignore that. "Is Skye around?"

"No, she's out with Timmy and her sister tonight."

"Oh."

"Try not to look so unhappy about that, will you?" Cole rolls his eyes. "I'm the one who's technically flesh and blood."

I aim a kick at his shins as I walk past. We might be older now, but he'll always have it coming. "I'm unfortunately aware of that, yes."

I hop up on one of the barstools and reach for a muffin from the center basket. Ever since Cole married Skye, there's always good food in the house. It's one of the many, many positive changes she's wrought on my brother.

"Skye texted me about the skiing weekend," I say, "three weeks from now. I'm guessing you closed on the place in Whistler?"

Cole reaches for a muffin of his own. "Yes. It was the third link I sent you."

"You know," I say good-naturedly, "a lot of billionaires will buy their own islands in the Caribbean. You couldn't be *that* kind of billionaire, could you?"

My brother gives me an amused glare. "No. That's for egomaniacs and James Bond villains."

"But an eight-room chalet nestled deep in the snowy mountains isn't?"

He flicks his muffin liner over to my side. "One more word and you're uninvited."

"You wouldn't dare. Skye would have your head."

"Unfortunately very true." He reaches for yet another muffin. "How's work going?"

"Good," I say. "I'm cautiously optimistic."

The glare he shoots me this time is tired. "You have to stop being cautious at some point, Blair. You're never cautious in any other area of your life."

There's truth to his words but I ignore them, spinning around on the barstool instead. Ever since my fashion brand spectacularly crashed and burned—so spectacularly that it was still used as an example in the media of what *not* to do—talking about my career dreams hurt. Better to work in silence than let people see me fail a second time.

"You're probably right," I admit.

"*Probably?*"

"It's the best I can give you," I tell him. "Remember, I'm programmed to oppose you at every turn. That's what a little sister does."

"Yes, and don't I know it," Cole says. "But put that on hold for just five minutes, okay? I've had an idea." There's a warning in his voice. "And before you bite my head off, let me just say that I genuinely think this might be good."

"What did you do now?"

"I didn't *do* anything, but I... well, I suggested something to Nick and he agreed."

I look up at him. "To Nick?"

"Yes. He's just bought a clothing giant. It's a pretty massive deal, actually. He needs to hire a consultant to advise with the retail and fashion side. You could be that consultant. You know the industry."

I put my purse down on the kitchen island with a bang. "Work for Nick?"

"For Nick's company, yes." Cole glances over at me. "Unless you find it too distasteful. He's probably slashing jobs right this moment to ensure they're profitable enough for as long as he needs them to be."

My fingers dance over the hem of my skirt. "You said Nick agreed?"

"Yes, he did. It was practically his idea."

My raised eyebrow must have been question enough, because my big brother rolls his eyes. "All right, so it wasn't. But I know you'd be great at this, Blair. What do you have to lose?"

Ah.

What he really means is *what do I have* left *to lose.* After my failed attempt at a fashion line, of course I'd jump at this chance.

"And you're certain Nick agreed," I say slowly. It makes no sense to me. Why would he entertain the idea for more than a second? The man has zero belief in my abilities.

"Yes, he did."

That's when it dawns on me—Nick doesn't think I can do it. He agreed because he bet on *me* being the one to turn it down.

I put on the brightest smile possible. If nothing else, accepting will annoy the hell out of him. "Of course I'll do it. I'll give him a call right away."

Cole's smile is wide. "Perfect. And who knows, perhaps the two of you will finally get to know one another better?"

My smile doesn't even falter. "Yes, who knows?"

Nick doesn't pick up the phone himself. I speak to his assistant instead, a no-nonsense man with an equally no-nonsense tone of voice. He pauses briefly when I introduce myself.

"Porter?" he says in clarification. "*Blair* Porter?"

"Yes."

"All right. I'll run it by Mr. Park immediately and get back to you within the hour."

He calls me back within ten minutes, and this time, his voice is nothing short of glacial. Whatever Nick's reaction was, it certainly hasn't warmed his assistant toward me.

I wish I could have seen it. Did he dramatically sweep all his things off his desk in a fit of anger? Or perhaps brood coldly, his hands white-knuckled around the edge of his desk?

"Mr. Park is glad you accepted," his assistant lies coolly. "You're welcome to come into the office tomorrow morning. We'll send you more detailed instructions by email within the hour."

My head spins as I hang up the phone. The decision to agree had been impulsive—driven by the desire to tell Nick off, to show him up. To beat back against his belief that I'm nothing but a socialite and a failed fashion designer.

I push back from the desk in my home office and look around at my mood boards, at the rack of samples in the corner. Above my desk is a framed quote. *Work in silence, let success be your noise.* The next time I launch a brand, it will be quietly. It won't have my name on it. And it *will* be a success.

I run a hand over the smooth silk of a slip skirt. Solutions for everyday women, that's my concept. Making the clothes you already own look good—no need to buy more. Extensions for bra straps. No-line panties. Beautiful T-shirt bras and shapewear and sneaker socks. Everything for the modern woman's closet, available to order online, in beautiful packaging. Well, it will be available, once it's launched.

But it'll have to wait a little while longer—long enough that I can show both my brother and Nick that I've still got it.

There's something about confronting a man you know dislikes you. It's reckless power and churning nerves and fire in my stomach. It's made worse still, somehow, when it's a man you once harbored a stupid crush on. That crush is *long* gone by now —driven away by his consistent harshness and dismissal. Whittled away by comments about my status as a trophy invite and inveterate shopaholic.

But I've never been one to back down, and when it comes to Nicholas Park, it's not even an option. That would mean surrender, and surrender means defeat, because that's the only language a man like him understands.

So I show up bright and early the next day at his office. Located in a mid-rise in downtown Seattle, it's nothing like the shiny skyscrapers my brother prefers.

A simple sign by the front door, so small you'd miss it if you didn't know you were looking for it.

Park Incorporated.

I've dressed for the part, my clothing my armor. My hair is glossy and blonde down my back and the belt of my trench coat is double-knotted around my waist. One fashion consultant at your service, *Nick.*

I'm greeted instead by a no-bullshit woman in her midforties. A faint frown mars her features.

"You're Blair Porter," she points out.

It's not a question, but I nod regardless. "Yes, that's me."

"I'm Gina Davies, hello. Mr. Park told me to expect you. Let's get you set up and briefed. I'm told you have a background in fashion and business?"

"I do, yes. A bachelor on the subject and two internships, not to mention personal business experience." I meet her unflinching gaze. If she's aware of the fiasco of my former fashion brand, I can't tell.

"Excellent. Here's your desk. I expect you'll be visiting different stores or working while traveling, but while you're here, this is yours." She pushes a thick file over to me and a laptop bag. "Here is all the information you'll need on B.C.

Adams. Mr. Park will brief you himself this afternoon, but for now, get acquainted with the firm."

"I'm already fairly well acquainted," I say, sinking down in the seat. "I used to be a regular customer."

It's meant as a lighthearted comment, but Gina seems to take it seriously. "Then maybe you can see why they've been failing to attract customers for the last decade. We need to turn that around if we're to get rid of the inventory and assess their production value."

I give a nod and open the binder carefully. "And Nick will see me this afternoon?"

"*Mr. Park* will, yes." She pushes away from the desk. "I'll let you get settled in. Tomorrow we visit the closest store."

And that's all the introduction I get.

But as I dive deeper into the documents I've been given, it's not hard to see the structural flaws of the business. Their retail model is dated; no online store, no shipping. The clothes they're selling are of good quality, and they're preppy, but they're *plain*. There's no clear branding. There's no logo.

No wonder they're struggling.

I'm so deep into research that I barely hear the knock on the door. It's Miles, Nick's assistant—I recognize the glacial voice immediately.

"Mr. Park will see you now."

I push away from the desk and deliberate for a moment over whether to bring the binder. Miles sees me considering and gives a faint sigh.

"Bring it," he says, turning on his heel and striding down the corridor without checking if I'm following.

Okay then. Nick's company probably doesn't score highly on the "employee satisfaction" index, but then again, I hadn't expected it to with him as the founder.

His office is on the other side of the complex. For a moment, I amuse myself by imagining him instructing Gina in the placement of my desk. *I don't care where she is, but make sure she is as many feet away from me as possible. Yes, I want you to measure it.*

22

Miles stops outside a closed door and presses down on the button of an intercom. "Miss Porter is here for you."

"Send her in."

I grin at Miles, hoping to draw out some form of response from him. All the employees here can't be ice-men. "Thanks for escorting me here," I say brightly.

He gives me a narrowed glance, as if he can't quite figure out my game, and pushes the door open. Oh well. I'm sure I'll wear him down eventually.

Nick is standing by a window, his back to me. The only one I've never managed to wear down with my charm. The door closes behind me. *Locked in with the beast.*

"Lovely office you have here," I say. "The mood seems to be somewhere between a slaughterhouse and a prison. I can't decide which I'm leaning toward more."

Nick doesn't turn. Dressed in black suit pants and a dark shirt, sans jacket, he looks… impressive. I know he's trying to rattle me by not speaking—by not looking at me.

I hate that it's working.

"Cole told me it was your idea to hire me. I'm guessing that was somewhat of a white lie, but I'll go along with it if it'll make your life easier."

Nick shrugs, his wide shoulders rising and falling once. "Believe what you like," he says, "as long as you'll do the job I've hired you for."

At that, my hackles rise. Have I ever suggested otherwise?

"So far, all I know is that it involves evaluating B.C. Adams as a business." I take a seat opposite his desk, ignoring the fact that he's also ignoring me. "I've been given a file about their financial information. That's all I know. Care to fill me in?"

Nick turns to look at me. There's still nothing in those dark eyes of his—he's capable of looking so cold, so still, like someone carved him from marble with too rough a hand. I sit still under the hawk-like gaze.

"And?" he says. "Do you think you can do it?"

"Yes." I pour more confidence into the word than I feel. "But I want you to tell me the truth about last weekend."

Impossibly, he grows even more still. "Last weekend?"

"Mr. Adams? B.C. Adams? I'm not an idiot. That was why you were there. You used my presence and my name for this deal."

Nick strides to his desk, pulling out his chair with one smooth motion. "And?"

"*And* that means I helped you close this deal."

He snorts. He actually *snorts*. "Not in the least. It was basically signed and sealed before."

"So you're saying you played cornholes with me voluntarily?"

His eyes narrow. "Fine. You're right on both counts. They had doubts, and seeing me as a person with friends, especially famous and well-liked friends, helped. Does that change the current situation in any way?"

"Not in the least," I say brightly, "but I very much wanted to hear you say it." I look away from the fire in his eyes to the binder in front of me. "Now, will you brief me on this job?"

Complete silence again. Nick is staring at me with clear frustration on his features. It's like he can't believe I'm really here.

That makes two of us.

"I didn't expect you to say yes," he mutters.

"Yes, well, I surprised myself as well. Now come on. Explain this process to me. What exactly have I been hired to do?"

Nick leans back in his chair. In this office, in his suit, everything about him speaks of boardrooms and spreadsheets and ruthless endurance. I've heard of this side of him before, but I've never seen it in action.

"They're deep in the red," he says. "Bleeding cash. Without our added liquidity, B.C. Adams would have gone bankrupt within the month."

My mind reels at the words.

And he bought companies on the brink like this *regularly?*

"Sounds like you should get your money back," I say. "Did you keep the receipt?"

He doesn't smile, but I didn't really expect him to. "We're sitting on a hell of a lot of inventory," he says. "They have two hundred and fifty stores across the country."

"Two hundred and fifty-three," I say.

He narrows his eyes at me again. "Two hundred and fifty-three," he concedes. "Gina has been calling store managers all morning. We're closing fifty of the least profitable locations immediately. They're setting up out-of-business sales as we speak."

My stomach drops. Fifty stores closed in a day, and all because he made the decision. How many employees had just been notified that they were redundant? How many families devastated?

Perhaps he sees these thoughts on my face, because Nick leans forward, a sudden flare of dark relish in his eyes. "It's only the beginning, Blair. Who knows how many stores we'll have to close before this is all said and done? I bought it to profit, not to save. Either I'll right the ship or I'll sell it off, piece by piece."

He wants to shock me.

He wants me to say that *I can't do it* and walk out of this office with my tail between my legs. It's there in his eyes, the challenge.

"Set up an online store," I say. "Immediately. The fact that they don't already have online shopping is beyond me."

A shadow of annoyance crosses his face. "We're trying to. Their stock is spread out between twenty different warehouses across the country."

"Inefficient," I say.

"*Very*," he says, looking more sullen about the fact that we're agreeing than the actual fact itself. "You'll work with Gina. She's running point on this. You can advise her on the retail side of the business. What inventory is sellable? What is unusable? Any ideas you have, she'll want to hear."

Despite the frown on his face—despite the fact that we're like vultures picking at a dying hundred-year-old American business —excitement unfurls inside me. My hands itch to sort through their inventory and their products.

"We're not selling to women like you." Nick holds up a warning finger. "This shop sells to the average woman. To… to housewives and teenagers."

"B.C. Adams does *not* sell to teenagers," I say tartly. "Which is why they're going out of business. And as for the target demographic, I'm perfectly capable of separating my own preferences from the market in general."

"See that you do." Nick's eyes gleam in the dim lighting of his office. I meet the challenge in his gaze squarely, ignoring the sudden racing of my heart. Perhaps my old crush isn't quite so dead and buried as I'd thought.

His next words are reluctant. "Welcome to the team, then."

4

BLAIR

Gina turns out to be no-nonsense personified. She works like a robot and very nearly talks like one, too. It's comforting—she doesn't openly doubt my capabilities but neither does she reassure.

"Here we are," she says as the cab pulls up outside of the B.C. Adams store in downtown Seattle. It looks like they all do—a familiar sign and a familiar layout. It's been many years since I'd stepped foot in one. Despite myself, Nick's voice comes back to me. *The target market isn't you.*

Could I really do this?

"Are you coming?" Gina waits by the automatic doors. I join her. Awaiting us is a store in complete disarray. A simple glance reveals a complete lack of thought to the layout of clothing racks, no artful display of clothing ensembles on mannequins. There's not a single customer in the entire store.

"Well," Gina says beside me. "This is going to take a bit of work?"

I feel like laughing at the understatement. Is that why Nick hired me? Because he expected me to give up, or worse still, fail spectacularly? Would that give him satisfaction?

"Unfortunately, yes," I say. "So let's dive right in."

For the coming hour, we make a list of everything we need to change. My hands fly across my phone as I take notes. *Re-organize sale section. Push inventory that skews younger to the front. Create a new marketing campaign.* Shown around the back by a friendly employee, Gina and I make a survey of all the inventory.

And it's a lot.

"Why did they stock four hundred and fifty orange T-shirts? There's no logo on it. It's quite literally just an orange T-shirt for grown women."

For the first time since meeting her, Gina's eyes crinkle in amusement. But her tone is professional. "Some women probably like it."

"Some probably do," I concede, "and more power to them. But ordering this huge quantity of them is crazy."

"If they'd been good at business we wouldn't be here," she says, heading into the next aisle. And so it continues. By late afternoon, my head is spinning with all the ideas we've discussed for restructuring the store.

My mind runs further ahead still—to a complete revamp of the entire brand. Commissioning a new logo and a new marketing profile entirely. I'll have to talk to Nick about how much money he's willing to put into this project. One thing is for sure, however. It'll cost money to make money with this store.

Gina and I don't leave until the store closes. My phone is filled to the brim with pictures of racks and clothing and inventory.

"We'll create a set of guidelines for changes tomorrow," Gina says, "and then we'll present it to Mr. Park."

I nod, hoping my voice sounds more confident than I feel. "Sounds great."

The cab ride to my brother's new house is one of deep contemplation. My hands play with the belt of my trench coat, thinking of tomorrow. Of standing in front of Nick and presenting my ideas. Of his dark eyes, which have never looked at me with anything but disapproval or indifference.

It doesn't matter, I tell myself. I'm doing this to prove something to him, yes, but mostly to myself and to my brother. That I'm not a quitter. That I'm more than my failed clothing line. That I'm not just the glorified socialite Nick thinks I am.

The cab drops me off outside of the giant wrought-iron gate to Cole and Skye's house in Greenwood Hills. I type in the passcode and head up the driveway, walking along a carefully landscaped path. Seeing the giant house now, it strikes me again just how much my brother's life has changed compared to only two years ago. An inveterate bachelor since his disastrous break-up, he'd shown no permanent interest in women until Skye.

Now he has a house and a wife. He's home in time for dinner in the evenings, not slaving away at a desk. I might tease him that she's completely tamed him, but truth be told, I'm more grateful to Skye than I could ever say for granting my brother happiness.

I ring the doorbell and try the handle simultaneously. It swings open. "It's just me!" I call, sinking down into one of the chairs artfully placed in the hallway.

"I can see that." The voice is deep and gravelly and not at all what I expected. Nick stands by the staircase, arching a dark eyebrow as he sees me struggling out of my thigh-high boots. I'd put them on impulsively this morning, but after a whole day on my feet, they've betrayed me. My feet are killing me. "Do you always get undressed in your brother's hallway?"

"I'm just taking off my shoes," I say tersely. "I didn't know you'd be here, *boss*."

Nick snorts. He's as aware as I am that the epitaph is not meant in a positive way. "I didn't know you'd be here, either," he says. "Would have skipped on dinner if I had."

The silence between us stretches on. I work the zipper down on my right boot but can't quite get it over my heel. My feet have probably swollen in the damnable things too, for all my luck, and I'm stuck here in front of the most intimidating man I know with my boots around my ankles.

He watches, relentless. "Struggling?"

"No, I'm fine."

I tug so hard that my knuckles whiten but the boot barely moves an inch. The damn thing is glued to my leg. I try wiggling the heel, but it won't budge.

"Fucking hell, just ask for help." Large, swarthy hands are on my ankle the next moment. Nick grips the bottom of my shoe with surprising gentleness and *tugs* and it slips right off.

He holds out his hands for my other leg and I lift it up, barely breathing as he undoes the zipper from knee to ankle. He yanks it off smoothly.

Embarrassment and an odd, tingly excitement are at war inside me. No doubt this is another strike in his Blair-isn't-capable column, or perhaps his I-only-see-Blair-as-Cole's-little-sister notebook.

He takes a step back and looks at my stockinged feet like they hold all the answers. I open my mouth to say *thank you,* but the arrival of my sister-in-law disrupts the moment.

Skye is beaming. "You're both here! Nick, have you been waiting for long?"

"Not at all," he says smoothly. For all my problems with him, I've never seen him be anything but unfailingly polite to my brother's wife.

Probably because he knows he'd be thrown on his ass if he ever slipped. Not that he's ever had such qualms with me.

Cole has his back to us, mixing drinks from the bar cart in the living room. He doesn't need to ask what we like.

Nick and I stand awkwardly side by side, waiting to be served our brandy and martini. Why have we both been invited to dinner? It's been months and months since the last time this happened.

"We've ordered in," Cole says. Skye shoots us a guilty look at that, but my brother just grins. "There was no time to cook. Besides, they cook better than we ever could."

"Taki's?" I ask.

"Farang," Cole says. "But good thinking with Taki. That'll be next time."

Skye takes a seat on one of the low couches and gestures for me to join her. "You two have started working together now, right? Tell us everything."

Oh no.

Is this why Nick and I have been invited? To report on our progress? I see the same pained realization in Nick's eyes, but he takes a sip of his whiskey, clearly leaving the answering to me.

"It's good," I hedge. "I mean, it's only been two days. I spent this one deep in the storage room of one of his stores, trying to sort through their inventory."

"And?" Cole asks, now sprawled in one of the armchairs. "Can they be turned around?"

My brother is asking, but Nick is the one observing me over the rim of his glass. Whatever I say will be commented upon tomorrow, no doubt.

"I think so," I say carefully, "but it's too early to tell. I think it'll be an expensive endeavor, though."

"Oh?"

My eyes flit to Nick's without my consent. They're narrowed, but with what emotion I can't tell. "Well, truly revamping their brand might include a new marketing campaign, new models, a new logo... I'm sure we'll talk about it more tomorrow."

Nick still hasn't acknowledged my words. He's just looking at me, and not knowing if it's in disapproval or interest makes me want to crawl out of my skin.

Cole snorts, turning to Nick. "Good thing you bought it when you did, man. Given another month, the Adams would have driven it into the ground."

"Most likely," he responds. "But they're also going around and giving interviews to any journalist who'll listen with their sob story."

"I saw that," Skye adds. "What did the *Wall Street Journal* call it? *'The American Gem'?*"

Nick nods, his lip curling in dark pleasure. "*'The American Gem falls prey to vultures,'* was the headline."

I wonder what it must be like to carry around the weight of

his reputation. To see yourself disparaged in a national newspaper like that, over and over again…

A phone rings from an adjoining room and Skye shoots up. "That must be the food."

My brother rises smoothly to his feet. Towering over Skye, he puts a hand on her lower back. "I'll help you carry."

And so Nick and I are again alone. I take a sip of the martini and look over at the fireplace. A framed picture of Cole and Skye on their wedding day hangs above it. The narcissists, I think, but not without fondness.

"An expensive endeavor, huh?"

My gaze flies back to Nick's. He's staring at me with a furrow between his brows. "Yes. I don't think it's impossible to make it profitable, but it'll need a revamp."

"And that's your professional opinion."

"Yes," I say slowly. "What else would it be?"

He glances past me, out toward the lake beyond and the glittering of houses that line it. "Why did you really accept this job?"

"Because you thought I wouldn't."

Nick actually smiles at that. It's not a smile of true happiness, and it's a slanted, crooked thing, but it's a smile nonetheless. "I was counting on the fact that you wouldn't."

"So I guessed. What, you didn't think I'd let you win just like that, did you?"

"A man can hope," he says. "So what? You accepted, and now you're going to deliberately sabotage my business? An *expensive* endeavor," he snorts.

Whatever wry amusement I'd felt flees. I put my glass down so hard I fear it might shatter. "You honestly think I'd do that?"

"Just to spite me? Sure."

I glare at him and will him to drop dead from the impact. But he doesn't, staring back at me like I'm his worst nightmare.

As if he wasn't mine first.

"Don't turn this around," I hiss. "I know you're hoping I'll fail, so you can go on believing I'm nothing but Cole's screw-up sister. Well, I won't. I refuse to."

"*Hoping you'll fail?* I have millions of dollars on the line here. Don't flatter yourself, Blair."

"Oh, I seldom do where you're concerned." I wrap my arms around my chest. "We don't need to like each other."

"Thank God," he mutters.

I pretend like the barb doesn't hurt. "What we do need to do is work together. And be civil, for their sake." I nod toward the door where Cole and Skye had disappeared. "Think you can do that, *vulture?*"

If he's offended by my use of his media epitaph, he doesn't show it. He extends a hand instead.

Once before I've shaken that hand. I still remember what it felt like—the faint scarring on the inside of his palm that's intrigued me ever since.

I close my fingers around his. They nearly disappear in his firm grip. He shakes my hand twice, eyes boring into mine the entire time.

"Prove me wrong," he says. "Help me make this business a success and I'll be civil."

"Fine," I grind out. "To civility and profit."

"Civility and profit."

We nod to each other like we've signed an historic peace accord. In a way, we have. Never before have we openly acknowledged our dislike of each other. To have it stated so baldly makes something in me wither.

Apparently, there's a difference between knowing and *knowing*. I want to ask him why we never became friends in the first place. But the fierce look on his face keeps any such questions from surfacing. No doubt he'd bite my head off for it.

The door swings open and Cole steps through with two full bags. The scent of curry and spice wafts through the air. Despite my anger, my mouth waters.

His eyes flit between Nick and me. My brother is no idiot—

he can feel the icy temperature in the room. He steps past us and into the dining room instead.

"Come along, children," he says in a tired voice. "If you'll stop bickering for just another hour, we'll let you out of here soon enough."

I don't know if Nick feels chastened, but I do. I'm on my best behavior all through dinner. Not surprisingly, that means largely ignoring Nick's presence.

"We're going to Whistler the weekend after next," Cole says. "There's more than enough room for both of you."

"In separate wings?" I quip.

"Thanks," Nick says, "but—"

"Oh, please, both of you, don't say no right away," Skye interjects. "There's space aplenty, not to mention a hot tub. We can play charades. Or," she adds, probably seeing the look in Nick's eyes, "we can spend the days skiing and the evenings quietly reading books and not talking at all."

Cole shakes his head at her rambling, but his smile is good-natured. He looks at us both. "I'd very much like you both to come," he says simply.

His words are enough to make my insides knot. I want to go. I want to spend time with them. I want to play charades and eat s'mores and doze by the fire.

Skye puts a hand on mine. Her eyes, so familiar and dear to me now, sparkle with mischief. "And you can bring the cute guy you're dating. André, right?"

I open my mouth to tell her that it's over—I'd broken that off nearly a month ago—but another voice speaks first.

"I'll go," Nick states. "Thank you for inviting me."

I look at him across the table. There had been no hiding the strength of purpose in his voice. "Lovely," Skye says. "We're happy to have you. The place is gorgeous, really."

"I'm sure it is." He glances over at me, as if he's daring me to accept.

I grit my teeth. "I'll come too," I say sweetly. "I can't wait."

"Me neither." Nick punctuates his words by attacking his

34

food a bit too strongly. Cole notices—damn my brother for never once being perceptive except *right now*. I don't want to be cross-examined later about our weird dynamic.

"So," I say brightly, reaching for the giant bowl of rice, "what's with all the food? Did you order enough to feed an army?"

Cole nods. "The fifth infantry division will be here in half an hour."

"Not exactly," Skye says. "We couldn't decide between dishes. And maybe…" She trails off, her eyes flitting to my brother's, and the instant communication that passes between them makes me feel like an imposter.

A quick glance at Nick tells me he feels the same way. They're wrapped up in a two-ness and domestic bliss that we're nothing but spectators to. For my sake, it makes me envious.

I'm sure Nick thinks it's ridiculous.

"Well, we didn't just ask you both here tonight to torture you," Cole says. "We do have something to tell you."

My throat closes. His words have sent my mind racing ahead, drawing conclusions, guessing. Cole's smile widens when he sees the hint of emotion in my eyes.

"You've bought another chalet?" Nick asks, and I hear his voice through some sort of fog. *No, you stupid man.*

Cole laughs. "Not quite. Almost, though."

"You're our closest friends and family," Skye adds, "and we feel like we *have* to share it with you. But no telling anyone else, okay? Not even your mother, Blair. Cole will tell her this weekend."

I'm nodding like a crazy person. "Of course, of course, I won't say a word."

"What is it?" Nick asks, a surprising trace of concern in his voice. "Is something wrong?"

"I'm pregnant," Skye says. "It's early still, but… we should be parents seven months from now."

My gaze becomes hazy with tears. I'm so happy for them, and I tell them that, going around the table to wrap my arms around them both. I don't know who to hug first and we end up in a sort of half-embrace, Skye laughing and me crying.

"I'm so happy for you," I say, perhaps once, perhaps twice. Perhaps a hundred times.

Cole finally pries me off his poor wife, now with tears of her own in her eyes, and hugs me tightly. I can't remember the last time we've hugged like this. "You're going to be a dad," I whisper in his ear.

"I know," he whispers back. "Think I'll do a good job?"

"Oh, the best." The thought of him as a father brings a fresh bout of tears to my eyes. "And I'll be an aunt."

Through my film of tears, I catch sight of Nick. He's standing to the side and watching the scene with an indecipherable emotion on his face. He gives Skye a quick hug. "Congratulations," he says.

I blink away my tears to see him more clearly. Is he moved, too?

Cole releases me with a grin. "You know what this means, right?"

"What?"

"We're going to ask you two to be godparents, when the day comes. You have seven months to prepare."

And then I'm hugging them again and my tears won't stop and I promise to be the best aunt and godparent ever. Skye laughs when she hugs me and asks me to come with her to buy baby clothes. *As if you could keep me away*, I say.

Nick looks… well, the only word I can use is shell-shocked. Cole pulls him in for a half-hug, their shoulders touching, and speaks. I can't hear it—but Nick gives a sharp nod. He's my brother's best friend. Of course he'd be asked. Even my anger at him melts away in the face of that.

Nick's shocked expression stays with me for the rest of the evening, even when we're sent off in the same car. Cole's driver greets us from the front seat as he pulls out from the driveway.

Nick is a quiet, dark shadow beside me.

"Wow," I murmur, more to myself than to him. "*Wow*."

He seems to agree. "Another project we're stuck on together."

There's no malice in his voice, and I laugh, despite myself. I'm still hurt by his belief that I wanted to sabotage his company, but that feels small and petty in comparison.

"I have a feeling I'll enjoy this one more," I say.

"Somehow, I was thinking quite the opposite," he says quietly.

"I don't know if I should take that as a compliment or be concerned for the child."

Nick doesn't respond. He looks down at the heavy watch on his wrist instead before leaning forward toward Charles. "Drop Miss Porter off first," he instructs.

"Yes, sir."

I frown at him. Is he going somewhere after? Something within me sinks when I think of how little I know of his personal life. Nothing of his relationships—or lack of them. Nothing of how he spends his time, or indeed, with whom.

"We don't talk about this tomorrow at work," he tells me.

"I wasn't planning to."

"Good. And remember our agreement."

Civility and profit. I turn my gaze away from him and out to the Seattle lights. I have a job to do, my own business to start, and now a niece or nephew on the way. Being disliked by Nick should be at the very bottom of my concerns.

"I won't forget," I vow.

5

BLAIR

History repeats itself the very next weekend.

I'm standing with a few friends, a glass of wine in hand. This event—a yearly autumnal fundraising event—draws a giant crowd. My brother *used* to be a regular guest, but he and Skye bailed last minute. When I'd asked him why, he'd laughingly said they needed to decide on a color for the nursery. *At nine o'clock in the evening?* He'd known it was an excuse, and I'd known it, but he'd sounded so content on the phone that I'd just wished him good luck.

My brother, a father.

I've spent the better part of this week thinking through what kind of aunt I want to be. I think I've settled on fun—that's key—but still with authority. Fun but kind. Someone the kid can call, during those inevitable teenage years, when they're in trouble but too afraid to go to Cole or Skye.

"Blair?" Maddie's voice reaches me and I force my eyes to refocus. "We lost you for a while there."

"Oh, I'm sorry. Just a lot on my mind."

"You've started working on something, I've heard." John leans against the bar table with a sly light in his eyes. "Will you *please* put us out of our misery and tell us what fantastic new project you're debuting?"

"An art exhibition, curated by the one, the only, Blair Porter?" Maddie intones. "Or perhaps a new Porter hotel, decorated by the fashionable Blair."

The group laughs and I make myself laugh along. "Good guesses, but no. I think I'll have to keep it to myself for a little while longer," I say, taking a coy sip from my drink.

"Oh, put us out of our misery!"

"I think you should suffer a bit more," I tease. In truth, I don't see the point in making it public knowledge that I'm working for Nicholas—ever. It'll raise questions, and I fear the convoluted logic won't make sense to anyone but myself, and possibly him.

Tate raises an eyebrow. "Are we finally going to see your comeback as a designer, Blair?"

A chorus of *oohs* and *aahs* erupt amongst the group. I force a carefree smile on my face. "You'll just have to wait and see."

"You can't even tell me? For old times' sake?"

I roll my eyes at him. We'd been classmates in high school, had even dated for a hot minute, but now we're nothing but polite acquaintances. "For old times' sake, I believe I still owe you a slap for homecoming. Who ditched me?"

His smile widens. "You're welcome to cash in anytime. I was a fool."

"I'll keep that in mind," I say dryly, my eyes drifting from his to the mingling guests behind him. There are a lot of familiar faces here tonight. Swirling my wine in my glass lazily, I listen with half an ear as Maddie launches into a discussion about a friend.

"He's terribly distraught," she says. "It's his family business being butchered, you know."

"Well, they sold it," John says. "The least they can do is watch."

"Who are we talking about?"

"Bryce Adams," Maddie replies. "I think you met his father at the Spencer wedding?"

Something sour burns in my throat. "Yes. Yes I did. He's distraught?"

"Park bought B.C. Adams," Tate says. "Though I'm sure you already know that."

They all chuckle, aware of the connection between Nick and Cole as well as the well-documented fact that Nick and I don't get along. I take a sip of my wine and ignore the flipping of my stomach.

The cuts Nick had made in the last week were extreme. Another forty stores slashed countrywide. All stock heading to one central location to make it easier for online sales. He was trying to salvage a shipwreck.

Surely they had to see that? I wet my lips, wondering if there's anything I can say on the matter.

"And speaking of the devil…" John says, his voice trailing off.

Maddie's voice is incredulous. "He never comes to these events."

"Don't know why he's started to," Tate mutters. "Is fundraising a business to pillage too?"

"You're just jealous," John tells him. "He's gotten *very* rich off pillaging. We all know your trust fund is wearing thin."

"Yes, that's absolutely it. I'm annoyed at my own morality."

I'm barely listening to their nonsense. My eyes are scanning the crowd, searching for a tall frame and closely cropped hair. For a man with a perpetual scowl and the build of a fighter.

I find him leaning by the bar. His dark suit follows his form closely, revealing the cut of his shoulders and length of his legs. A glass of brandy dangles from his fingers. The eyes he sweeps over the gathered guests are just as impassive as usual.

And that's when I realize I've never really seen Nick in any environment where he belongs. He's permanently apart, uneasy, different. Is there anywhere he simply *exists*?

He turns his head toward me. Our eyes meet.

It must be twenty feet between us, but I can see his raised

eyebrow as if he were standing right next to me. He inclines his head slightly, no more than an inch, but it's a greeting.

I give a shallow nod. The past week has been excruciatingly civil. We've rarely worked together, as I report to Gina, but the times we've been in the same room have been like some deranged adaption of Austen. *Yes, thank you. No, thank you. Yes, please, sir. I'll bear that in mind. Would you kindly?*

We haven't spoken a single word to each other that's not work-related.

"Blair?"

I tear my gaze away from Nick's dark one. "Yes?"

"Are you angrier with him than usual?" Maddie's voice is concerned. "You looked so…"

"Distraught," Tate says.

The smile that spreads across my features is genuine this time. "Not at all. I didn't mean to zone out." I turn my back to Nick. The same Nick who recently admitted that he doesn't like me—who only offered me a job because he thought I'd turn it down.

Funny how ignoring someone is an active thing. I have to force myself to stop my constant awareness of him. Even when I try not to, my body knows where his is as he makes his way through the party.

I catch him talking to a brunette in a beautiful beaded dress. Her hand drifts to his arm twice—and neither time does he move away. I grip my glass of wine firmly and try to ignore my irritation.

It's a common occurrence, this. Women are attracted to him because of his money or his terrible reputation, just like Maddie had a few weeks earlier.

He catches me when I head to the bar for a refill. Stepping neatly into my path, Nick moves more gracefully than one would imagine a man of his height and build might.

"Blair."

I wet my lips. "Nick."

"You've abandoned your group of admirers." His gaze

flickers over my head to something in the distance before returning to me.

"*Friends,*" I correct him.

"Lackeys," he continues. "Posse. Leeches. Take your pick."

I shift my weight. "And the woman you were talking to earlier wasn't just interested in your wealth?"

"Of course she was," he says smoothly. "And I'm not the least bit deluded about it."

"Neither am I." But even as I say it, his words from the Spencer wedding come back to me, when he'd told me I was a trophy invite.

"Of course not," he drawls. "You probably know everyone in this room, right? Blair Porter, invited everywhere, a friend to everyone."

The jab hits home. He's not saying it as a compliment—that much is clear. "Rather a friend to everyone than a friend to no one," I say sweetly.

"I'm not surprised you'd see it that way. Be careful, though. Your social standing is probably decreasing by the second, standing here talking to me." He sounds pleased by the thought.

I take a sip from my wine to buy myself time. "I didn't know you'd be here tonight," I say finally. "Fundraising doesn't seem like your scene."

"It isn't." His gaze flits above my head again. "Your *friends* are staring daggers at me, especially the weaselly-looking one. It's very amusing."

I resist the urge to turn around. "Ignore them."

"Now, why would they do that? Have you told them anything about me?"

"Nothing," I say truthfully. "I'm pretty sure your reputation precedes you in this case."

His eyes narrow. "Which one of them is André?"

I have to school my features to hide my surprise. He remembered the name of the last guy I'd dated? And then it hits me—Skye had mentioned him last weekend, at dinner. Invited him to the chalet, in fact.

42

"He couldn't come tonight," I say sweetly. It's not really a lie either. He couldn't come, on account of not having been invited.

Nick shrugs. "What a shame. I'm sure I would have enjoyed meeting him."

He would not *enjoy meeting you,* I think. "Really? That's an unusually nice sentiment from someone who's never nice."

"Nice," he snorts. "As if you've ever been *nice* to me."

And perhaps it's the two glasses of wine I've had, or the anger at his offhand comments, but I actually blurt the next words out. "You were rude to me first."

Even as I say it, I can hear how childish it sounds.

Nick doesn't seem to mind. He takes a sip of his brandy instead, a furrow in his brow. "You'll have to remind me."

"The poker game," I say, pushing my hair back behind an ear. "I asked to join and you turned me down in front of everyone in the room."

He looks shocked, but then he laughs. It's a dark thing. *"That?* I was saving you! Those guys were absolute assholes."

"As were you."

"As was I," he agrees. "As I said—*saving you.* That game was nothing for you. You were what, nineteen? And Cole's younger sister?"

"I'd just turned twenty-one." I cross my arms over my chest. If that had been his reason, there had been no reason to be rude —nor to be rude at every turn since. "Motivated by altruism? I'm sorry if I don't buy it."

Nick shakes his head. Not for the first time, I wonder if his nose has ever been broken. "I'm not surprised."

"I guess civility is only for work, then."

"That was our agreement, yes." He tips his glass of brandy in my direction, voice dripping with condescension. "Extending it to around the clock would probably be more taxing than you could manage."

Me? I'm the one who's only ever wanted to be his friend. I grit my teeth. "I'm going on that ski trip," I say fiercely.

If he's bothered by the non-sequitur, it doesn't show. "Oh, so am I," he counters.

"And I'm an excellent skier."

"As am I."

"Excellent."

"Perfect."

We stand there glaring at each other. My heart beats against my ribs, aware how much closer we're standing than when we began talking. Nick's eyes are dark flames. For the first time in years, I feel like he's looking at me and seeing *me,* not Cole's little sister. He might not like what he sees, but it feels like a victory regardless.

"Mr. Park!" A voice breaks us out of our staring contest. A portly man appears at Nick's side, a mustache hiding his nervous smile. Thomas York, head of the fundraising committee.

Nick's face smooths back into schooled impassivity so quickly that I wonder if I'd imagined the passionate irritation there. "Mr. York."

"I'm sorry to interrupt your, erm, discussion, but I was informed by your people that I was to find you as soon as possible. Well, here I am."

I watch in fascination as Nick nods. "Thank you for making the time. Let's talk. If you'll excuse me, Miss Porter…"

I produce my widest, most beaming smile. "Of course. It was a pleasure meeting you, Mr. York. And Mr. Park… do take care. I want you to be in perfect shape when I race you on the slopes."

Nick's eyes glitter in the dim lighting. "Prepare to lose," he says.

6

NICK

Whistler is a sight from the air. At my request, the helicopter makes an extra round before we descend over the snow-ladened landscape. Mountains stretch high around us, dark green pines barely visible beneath a blanket of heavy white.

It's one of the many sights I'm determined not to take for granted. Nor is international travel. The Canadian border might only be a two-hour drive from Seattle, but I'd never left the country until I was well into adulthood.

I force my mind away from the thought. It's easy to stray too close to childhood memories, and I'd rather not dwell on most of those.

The helicopter makes a smooth landing on the helipad. Kept free from ice and snow all year round, there's no quicker way to travel. If Cole were here, no doubt he'd make some quip about how it saves him time—and time is money. He's never truly appreciated this kind of thing, having grown up with money long before he made his own billions. Blair, despite her sunny nature, is the same. Both of them come from comfort. That was as clear as the privilege they'd been raised with.

They displayed it often, but never deliberately. It just hung around their shoulders like a cloak and shone through in their speech. In shared childhood memories of Caribbean cruises and ski trips.

The difference didn't feel insurmountable with Cole. It never had. But with Blair? It had been a sign over her head from the first time I saw her. NOT FOR THE LIKES OF YOU. Hell, I'd added to that monument myself over the years. Little roadblocks and diversions. Cues to say the thing she'd least like hearing.

And the difference between us grew until it became a mountain.

Unbidden, my mind conjures up the image of them both when we'd been told about the pregnancy. Cole was happy, in that deep, content way, and good for him.

Blair had *cried*. She'd actually cried, happy, warm tears that she wasn't the least bit ashamed about shedding. Joy had illuminated her from within, leaving her practically glowing, as she hugged them both. She wore her emotions on her sleeve.

It's been nearly two weeks, but the memory still hits me every now and then. Never had I seen her so happy. It wasn't a face she generally showed around me.

No, with me she's a hissing cat. Teeth bared and hackles raised. It's predictable and safe, at least. Easier by far to face.

A car is waiting for me by the helipad. The driver makes his way in silence up the snowy streets of Whistler, passing chalet after chalet on the mountainside. Cole and Skye should already be there, having flown up a day earlier. I suspect Blair had gone with them.

A job that's respected. A wife who adores him. A child on the way and nothing but a good life to lead. For a moment, I nearly drown in my own bitter envy of Cole. It doesn't happen often—I couldn't be the man if I tried—and it doesn't last long.

When the car stops outside a chalet that's as much window as it is pine, my indulgence in self-pity is over. The house is nestled in a snowy hillside and entirely surrounded by firs. I take the steps in two and let the staff handle my luggage.

Cole stands by the front door. Wearing a woolen sweater and

with at least a few days of unshaved growth on his face, he looks like he's given up entirely. He's also grinning widely.

"Christ, man," I say. "Are you trying to become one with the mountain?"

He pulls me in to slap me on the shoulder. "Yes. Perhaps then it'll stop seeing me as an enemy."

"An enemy?"

"He took a fall today!" Skye calls from behind him. "While skiing!"

"It wasn't all that bad," Cole says.

"Nothing broken, I hope?"

"Nothing vital at least. Come on, see the place." I follow him into a large living space. White couches and sheepskin throws make way to a gigantic copper fireplace. The entire north-facing facade is glass, and the view is just as spectacular as I suspected. All of Whistler and the snow-covered mountains beyond.

"It's so beautiful, isn't it?" Skye is sitting on one of the couches, a thick bathrobe around her. She's cupping a mug in her hands. "There's a deck, too, with a hot tub. You can head out there now, if you'd like. Relax from your traveling."

The idea of some peace and quiet and hot water wins. It doesn't take long to get installed in one of the guest rooms and then I'm making my way out into the cold winter air in nothing but my trunks.

The hot tub is illuminated by underwater spotlights. Steam rises from it into the freezing air, snow melting around it.

Only it's not empty.

Blair is sitting with her back to me. Only her shoulders and neck are visible above the water—smooth, tan skin. Her wheat-blonde hair is swept up into a messy pile on her head, tendrils hanging down her neck. They curl in the steam.

"You're back," she says languidly. "I've come up with some new names in the meantime. Before you laugh, let me tell you why I *genuinely* think Bear could be a cool name. At least as a middle name."

I walk around the edge of the hot tub. "It's a good name, *if* you don't care about the kid. Are you trying to get them to revoke their offer of being a godparent?"

Blair's eyes widen as she takes me in. For just a second, I can almost convince myself that a happy welcome is coming.

But then she frowns. "I didn't hear you arrive."

"If you were out here the whole time, that would have been impossible, yeah." I step into the hot, bubbling water. The tub is large enough that there is plenty of distance between us, but it still feels like a bad idea. The past few weeks have put her more squarely in my path than before—sometimes by my own doing.

It's a disaster waiting to happen.

"I haven't been here the *whole* time," she says. "I've been skiing today, too."

"Hitting the blacks?"

Her eyes drift closed. Two thin black bikini straps rise from below the water to tie around her neck. "No, Cole and I skied the reds today."

"Skye didn't?"

"No," she says. There's no antagonism in her voice, no anger or frustration. She sounds like does when she's speaking to her brother or her friends. It's deceptively easy to think I'm the latter. I shift in the water, not wanting to disturb her.

"Why not?"

"She's pregnant, you dolt," Blair says. "She sat out here with me earlier, but could only have her legs in the water. Apparently you can't go in the hot tub while you're pregnant, either. Did you know that?"

The subject isn't overly interesting, but her voice is, warm and confidential. A small lock of blonde hair is curling at her temple.

"No."

"We googled and made a list," Blair continues. "You can't sauna, either. Drink coffee. Eat sushi or certain kinds of cheeses. No rare meat. You shouldn't wear heels. You can't drink."

"The last one seems fairly obvious."

Her eyes glitter with amusement. "Yes, well, I wanted to add it for good measure. It made the list longer. Comedic effect, you know."

"You could list all the illegal drugs she can't take, either, if you want to really hammer the point home." I glance past her to the snowy mountaintops above us. Cole's chalet is fairly isolated —no one can see us from here. It's not gated, but there aren't exactly any close neighbors, either.

"It's enough to make me reconsider having kids," she says. Her voice is jovial, but my eyes flit back to hers regardless.

"You need to find someone to have them with first," I point out. "Apparently André couldn't make it?"

She dips lower into the water until only her head and the tips of her shoulders are exposed to the cold air. "No, he couldn't."

"What a pity." I'd wanted to get a good look at the guy.

But Blair doesn't sound the least bit sad when she says, "Yes, very much so."

I rest my arms along the edges of the hot tub. The cold air bites at my skin, a sharp contrast to the warm, bubbling water below. It's the first time we've spoken about anything other than work-related topics since the charity event. "So what have you been doing? Torturing these poor souls with never-ending rounds of charades?"

Her eyes narrow into the expression I'm used to. Good. "No," she says. "I've barely even suggested it."

"Surprising." I lean my head back against the edge of the tub and glance up at the sky. The sun is starting to set, the clear sky darkening along its infinite edges.

"What did you discuss with Thomas York? At the charity event?"

I resist the urge to groan. "Have you ever had a thought you didn't speak out loud?" I ask. It's a nasty question. I don't look at her to see if the barb struck—the imagined hurt on her face is painful enough.

"Yes," she says tartly. "I'm having a lot of thoughts about you right now that I'm not going to speak out loud."

Looking up at the sky where she can't see it, I let my lips curl. The hackles are raised. "Restraint. How novel."

"I show it every day at work," she says. "Even you can't tell me I've been anything less than *perfectly* civil."

"You have," I admit. And despite myself, I'd found myself missing our spats during the robot-like exchanges we'd had about B.C. Adams. Blair avoided me like the plague, sending all her points through Gina.

Just like I'd asked her to.

"And you can't tell me I haven't done my job, because I know I'm doing it well."

Gina had expressed the same thought to me just yesterday. *You said she'd be untrained, sir, but so far her insights have mostly been spot-on.*

"We'll see," I say. "I still haven't turned a profit."

"You will," she says. "I've heard that Bryce Adams is devastated, by the way."

I tip my head forward to find her staring at me. There's a flush in her cheeks, from the heat or from the cold, and a challenge in her golden-brown eyes. No one else has her coloring—wheat and honey and chocolate, and not one inch of it fake.

"Have you spoken to him?" I ask.

"No. But our circles overlap."

Oh yes, her circle. All the people who hung around her for notoriety or for fame. Because she's often been the talk of the town—*billionaire Cole Porter's little sister, latest in a line of failed socialite entrepreneurs.* Excellent friends indeed.

"If he's so devastated, he shouldn't have run his family's legacy into the ground," I say evenly. "He has only himself to blame. Well, and his father. And grandfather."

Blair reaches up to run a hand over the back of her neck. Rising slightly from the water, the wet expanse of her chest and the curves of her breasts come into view. I force myself to look away and ignore the two black triangles that cover them from my view. "What will happen to all the employees you're terminating?" she asks.

Good, I think. Keep taunting me about things like this and I'll stop noticing your beauty in no time at all. "I don't know. That's not my problem."

Her eyes narrow. There's disapproval there. "They were *your* employees up until the day they were let go."

"Yes, and they were let go with the same terms and conditions that they agreed to when they were hired by B.C. Adams. Severance and all." My voice drops. "I'm not Thomas York. I don't run a charity, Blair."

"I know that." Her cheeks flush further—I know she hates being spoken to like I just did, with the tone of voice that implies she doesn't know any better.

"What you're really saying is that you're uncomfortable with the idea of working for someone like me," I say.

"No. I get why you have to fire people. It's just—"

"Immoral? Not the first time I've heard that." I let my gaze wander from her to the giant pines that encircle us, my expression bored.

She drops the discussion, but I don't feel the same rush of success as usual. *Keep going,* a voice whispers in my head. *Challenge me.*

"You claimed to be a good skier," she says instead. The tone of her voice is as cold as the nip in the air—the comfortable friendliness she'd shown me when I first sat down in the hot tub is gone. I did that, ruined her mood as surely as I ruin most things.

"I am," I say. Like most things in life, I'd started skiing late, far later than Cole and Blair—their jet-setting parents had sent them off with a ski instructor before they could walk.

Blair doesn't know that. "So am I," she says instead. "I'm looking forward to racing you tomorrow, then."

Ah. For some foolish reason, I'd expected Cole and me to go skiing together like we used to. Taunting each other to more daring pistes. The rush of reaching the bottom before him.

With Blair... I don't want her to push herself to go as fast as me. Scenarios play out in my head, of her flipping or careening and ending up with a broken limb. Her beautiful face marred in pain. Of me, explaining it all to Cole.

She mistakes my hesitation and shakes her head. "Fine. Be scared, then." But there's genuine confusion in her tone.

Fuck. Whatever I do or *don't* do with her is wrong somehow, and I know it's my fault.

It's always my fault.

"I'm heading inside." She rises from the steaming water. There's no hiding from the sight—from her body so very nearly unclothed. The black bikini hides almost nothing.

An expanse of dewy, honey-colored skin. A curved waist and full breasts and as she turns to climb out, long legs and a firm ass. Her body is as glorious as her face. I'd suspected that, for years. Having it confirmed makes my whole body tighten.

As if in a daze, I drag my gaze up from her taut stomach to the incredulity in her eyes as she catches me watching her. For a long moment, we just stare at each other across the steam of the hot tub.

Then she flushes, and this time it's not from the cold.

"Well," she says faintly, wrapping her towel tight around herself. And then she disappears inside, leaving me to my miserable thoughts and aching body.

7

BLAIR

Nick had checked me out. Practically ogled, and there had been no mistaking the hunger I'd seen in his gaze. It's the first time in the eight years I've known him that I've ever seen him look at me like a woman—like something other than Cole's spoiled little sister.

The look re-ignited my stupid old crush. Despite his words, the harshness of them, the constant comments. *Do you ever have a thought you don't speak?* Or once, two years ago. *Don't you have another failed fashion line to launch?* They'd hurt, and whittled away at my want of him. I'd thought it nearly gone.

But his gaze has brought it all back.

And more than that—I realize now that I have *power* where he's concerned. Not power he's willing to give up, but power all the same. A small part of him, at least, wants me.

The thought keeps me from sleeping. Lying in the giant bed in one of the guest rooms, I stare up at the pine-wood ceiling and ignore the stag horns mounted on the opposite wall. He's in a bed in a room not far from here. What's he thinking?

It's a stupid question. Not once have I been able to predict what Nicholas Park thinks, and starting now will drive me mad. But still.

He'd looked.

Skye and Cole are already up when I drag myself out of bed the next day. They're in the kitchen, Cole watching as Skye flips pancakes, her brown hair in a braid down her back. I watch them from the door for a moment. He's taunting her—saying she can't flip more than two in a row.

"My money's on Skye," I announce.

"Ah-ha!" she says. "At last, someone has confidence in me."

Cole shakes his head at me, but his smile is wide. "Et tu, Brute?"

"Especially me," I confirm. "Is Nick not up yet?"

"He's already down in town, getting his gear," Cole says. "He said something about hitting the slopes early. Is it all right if you two ski alone this morning? I'll join Nick out on the slopes later today."

"Of course. That means the afternoon is ours," I add to Skye. "There's a ton of non-skiing activities in Whistler, you know. We could go dog-sledding."

Her eyes light up. "I've always wanted to do that."

"Then you two should *definitely* do that." Cole is already reaching for his phone. "Let me call them and set it up. We went there when we were what, eleven and eight?"

I nod. "I'd just seen the movie *Balto*. It was epic."

"We should take Timmy dog-sledding when he joins us next time," Skye says. "He'll love it."

Cole steps away to set it up. I grin at Skye, and find her grinning right back at me. "Have I told you that I'm happy my brother married you?"

"Yes," she says, flipping another pancake high. Her smile is triumphant. "Including during your wedding toast. But I still very much like hearing it."

"Good, because I'll keep saying it."

The rest of the morning passes in a kind of lovely, vacationy haze, one that makes my muscles ache and my heart happy. Cole's chalet is staffed when he's there, and one of the drivers helps me assemble all the gear I'll need. I'm ready by the time Nick returns.

He takes a step back when he sees me waiting, leaning on my skis. We look like polar opposites—my trousers and ski jacket are sleek and white, his are form-fitting and black. The high neck of his jacket rises up to meet the cropped fit of his dark hair.

"You're ready," he says.

I nod. "Ready to race you to the end." This is something I know I can do. Sunscreen on, hair braided, my body itching to hit the slopes. Cole and I used to race, too—but he has Skye now. I suppose Nick might feel the same way. Both of us discarded, forced to race against each other.

"Let's go, then," he says darkly.

And we do.

By the time I join Skye for our dog-sled excursion, my legs feel like they're shaking with every step. The comfortable tiredness of a day of exercise, my skin tingly with the nip in the air.

Skye is bundled up in a giant puffy coat when I arrive. "They have puppies in the kennel," she tells me in an aside. "Think we can visit them afterwards?"

"We absolutely should." I wince as I climb into the sled. I'd fallen once, to my massive embarrassment, but Nick hadn't commented on it—just offered me his hand to get up. I'd been banking too hard. A rookie mistake, really.

Beneath his ski mask, I hadn't been able to see his eyes at all. But I'd raced him to the bottom not once, not twice, but three separate times, the last one on a black slope. He was a damn good skier, but I'd kept his pace, matching him stroke for stroke.

Skye and I return to the chalet with more than enough time before the guys get back. The shower is practically life-restoring. Warm water over my muscles, the smell of magnolia from my shampoo, and I'm a new woman when I emerge. Looking at myself in the mirror, I take my time as I put on body lotion.

The look on Nick's face as his gaze swept me head to toe in my bikini comes to mind. It makes my stomach tighten. I'd seen him in his swimming trunks, too, but I'd been too surprised to really *see* anything before he got into the tub.

Refusing to think about why I'm doing it, I slip into the best underwear I'd brought with me. A nude bra edged with lace, the cups slanted and flattering. A pair of matching seamless panties cut high on the sides.

Both of them are of my own design—a part of the new brand I'm working on, the one nobody will know is mine until I'm sure it's a success. Finally, I pull on a silk skirt and a cashmere sweater, sticking my feet in a pair of slippers.

By the time I make it back to the kitchen, the staff are already starting to set the table and prepare for dinner. I give them an excusing smile. "Is it all right if I bake something for dessert? I just need a small, tiny corner of the kitchen island."

I'm given ample space, though all I really need is a bowl and whisk. Chatting to Kristen, the hired chef, I start making the same brownie recipe that Mom always made when we were skiing. She'd sent it to me before this trip in exchange. Well, she'd tried to—the picture she snapped was blurry, but I could just about make out the measurements.

The kitchen smells amazing by the time they're in the oven. I'm leaning against the counter, listening to Kristen tell me stories about other chalets she's worked at in Whistler, when the front door opens.

Cole and Nick burst into the house like a tornado. Snow drips from their jackets, both of them grinning from ear to ear. It's the kind of smile I've never seen on Nick before.

"That last fucking slope, man… you had me." Cole sits down on one of the low benches and starts tugging at his snow boots. Opposite him, Nick does the same, leaning against a wall.

"Only because of the final turn. One more of those and you'd have won." Nick unzips his jacket and it falls to the ground behind him. The black polo-neck he's wearing underneath looks painted on him, tight against his wide chest and the curves of his shoulders.

My brother finally gets off his own jacket. "Too many *almosts* for my taste. Next time I'll have you."

"Well, you're welcome to try."

Cole stretches, his eyes finding mine. "Something smells amazing. Are you making *brownies*, Blair?"

"Yes." My eyes are locked on Nick, though. The smile he'd worn just prior is gone now.

Cole stops beside me to press a quick kiss to my cheek. "Good thinking. Don't forget to send Mom a picture of them later."

The suggestion would have made me smile, if I hadn't been drowning in the darkness of Nick's gaze. Am I the only one who's caught in this tension? Around me, the staff keep preparing dinner as if nothing is happening, my brother whistling as he disappears deeper into the house to find a shower of his own.

"Congratulations on your victory," I tell Nick.

"Thank you," he says quietly. "Enjoyed your time with the dogs?"

"Immensely."

"Good." And then his lip curls, just slightly. "Look at us being civil."

"I wonder how long it'll last," I say.

His gaze drops to my hands, knotted in front of me on the kitchen counter. We'd been good today, when all we had to do was ski. When the fire between us could be channeled into harmless competition.

I open my mouth to say just that when the alarm goes off. My brownies are done. I tear my gaze from his to take them out, forcing Ken, the kitchen assistant, to move. He gives me a lopsided smile when I apologize. "Let me taste one of those and all is forgiven," he says.

Behind me, Nick heads to his room, taking my chance to offer a nice comment with him. Watching the perfect brown squares of chocolate goodness in front of me, I barely register the smell.

"Are you *sure* no one else wants hot cocoa?" Skye asks hopefully. She's standing by the kitchen counter with a mug in her hands. Beside me, Cole is sitting with his whiskey, and in the couch opposite, Nick with his brandy.

I raise my glass of white wine. "I'm sorry, but I'm good."

"Seven more months of being the odd one out," she declares. "A small price to pay for an eternity of happiness, I suppose."

Cole snorts. "Remember to remind him of that when he's throwing temper tantrums as a teenager. 'You were supposed to be our eternity of happiness!'"

"But, you know, *no pressure*," I add.

Skye laughs. "We're screwing up this parenting thing already, and we're not even parents yet!"

"So we've nowhere to go but up," Cole says. "Just the way I like it."

From the couch opposite ours, Nick swirls his brandy in his glass. He'd been quiet most of the dinner, his attention most often on the falling snow outside of the giant windows. Now, his gaze seems locked on the roaring fire.

The question hovers on the tip of my tongue. *What are you thinking about?* Anyone else, I would have simply asked. Anyone else, and I would have given them a smile and a teasing joke. But he would never welcome it and I can't bring myself to ask it.

"What time is the helicopter ride tomorrow?"

"We leave here at nine," Cole says. "You're both joining, right?"

"Absolutely," I say. The tour he's booked is to a nearby glacier. The helicopter will land in the remote wilderness, a guide walking us along the ever-evolving landscape of ice and snow. Frozen slides, miles-deep crevices and deep-blue ice caves.

Nick nods too. "I'll be there."

It's not long before Cole and Skye decide to retire for the evening. *We'll play charades tomorrow,* Skye promises me, grabbing one last brownie.

"For the road," she tells me. "It's a big house, you know. I might get hungry on the way."

Nick doesn't move, and caught in indecision, I stay where I am, seated on one of the large couches with my legs folded up beneath me. The only sound in the living room is the crackling from the fireplace.

I make a decision. Maybe it's a stupid one, but I'm drawn in by the remoteness of his gaze, by the ridiculous confidence his ogling yesterday has given me.

I get up to fetch the deck of cards from the dresser nearby. Nick watches me as I put it resolutely on the table between us. "I think you owe me a round of poker."

Nick's eyes slide from the cards to mine. There's something burning in them, and I don't know if it's irritation or excitement or a deliciously heady mix of the two.

"You truly haven't forgotten that."

"Of course I haven't."

"Nor forgiven me, it seems." His voice grows gruffer. "I told you, I was doing you a favor."

"Play a game with me and I will." I split the deck in two with a flourish. This, I know how to do, courtesy of my brother. I begin to shuffle with practiced moves.

Nick watches me work in silence. "We have no chips," he says. "No stakes at all. That's hardly poker."

"We could raise them," I say. "Make it more... *interesting,* if playing for my forgiveness isn't interesting enough for you."

The harsh line of his jaw works. "You're not suggesting what I think you are."

"Sure I am."

"Strip poker?"

My heart is beating wildly against my ribs, but my hands remain steady. "Yes. A heads-up game, either five-card draw or Texas hold 'em. Come on. You owe me one, remember?"

He takes a deep sip of his brandy. Silence is heavy between us. "Fine," he says finally. "Five-card draw."

"All right." I shuffle the cards one last time before dealing five cards to each of us. He's wearing a pair of dark trousers and a gray sweater—two major articles of clothing, then.

"We're evenly matched," I comment.

His eyes drift over my form in one impassive sweep. Carefully controlled, with none of the heat I'd seen yesterday.

"So it would seem." His voice has deepened. "You're welcome to start the betting."

"You're that sure of yourself?"

"Perhaps."

I smile down at the two cards I've flipped. Two tens. Not bad. "My sweater is my ante."

"So is mine."

I don't exchange any of my cards before the river is dealt. He does, however, the back of his hand coming into view as he reaches for another card.

"Let's see, then…" I deal out the river and we both turn our hands. I have three tens, and he has a pair.

"Whoops," I drawl. "Seems like I won the first round."

Nick's eyes narrow at the cards, as if he's expecting them to change. But they don't, the evidence of my victory clear between us. A log in the fireplace snaps loudly behind him.

"So you did," he agrees darkly. Large hands reach down to grip the hem of his sweater, pulling it off. He's not wearing anything underneath. Just sun-darkened skin and a rough smattering of hair on his chest. Sculpted shoulders. A strong, taut abdomen.

It's the body of a man who works with it, who has strength because strength matters, and none of the superficial ab muscles that comes from crunches in a gym. What does he do to look like that?

I'm taking too long in responding. "Good," I say inanely. "Your time to start."

"I suppose my ante's my pants now," he says. There's dark

amusement in his voice. "Your brother better stay in his room, or he'll kill me for this."

The master bedroom is on another floor. There's zero risk of them coming out here, and the staff has all left. Even so, his words knot something inside of me.

"My ante's the same." I finger the hem of my soft sweater. I'm not wearing a T-shirt beneath it either—preferring the soft feel of cashmere against my skin. "You're not cold over there, are you?"

The gaze he shoots me is withering. "Deal, Blair."

"So bossy." I hand him the five cards needed. "Perhaps you need a bit more brandy to loosen up."

He shakes his head at me, but to my surprise he does what I suggested, tossing back what's left in his glass. "You'll eat your words tonight."

"I will?"

"Yes," he growls. "There was a reason I didn't let you join our poker game all those years ago."

A shiver runs down my back. He might talk a big game, and he certainly has a reputation, but I've never felt anything but safe around Nick. Even when he's tested my patience to its very limits.

This time, my one-pair is no match for his two-pair. "Damn," I say morosely, sitting back on my knees. "I guess we're even now."

"So we are." His gaze strays from my eyes to my neck as he speaks. The butterflies in my stomach erupt into a frenzy as I make a show of pulling off my own sweater. *He looked at you yesterday*, I remind myself. *He's not as cool as he pretends to be.*

I toss it aside and shake my hair out. It falls around my shoulders, the ends tickling along my back. "Well," I tease. "I guess we're both playing as skins now."

He reaches for the cards. "We're not evenly matched, though."

"Oh?"

"You have one more item of clothing than me." He inclines

his head toward me, even as his eyes stay focused on the cards in front of him.

Ah. My bra.

Before I let myself consider it, I reach back and undo the clasp with wan hands. The straps slide off my arms and I toss it off to the side.

"There," I say. "*Now* we're even."

8
NICK

"Fucking hell, Blair." I glance once and then away, my hand tightening around my cards. They bend in my grip.

"I won't let you claim that I won unfairly." She reaches for her cards with a level of nonchalance I can't relate to at the moment. "What? Did you think I was joking when I agreed to strip poker?"

The better question is, why on earth had I agreed to this?

And at the same time... seeing the expanse of her skin, honey and wheat and gold, *how could I not have?*

Her nipples are just as I'd imagined they'd looked yesterday, after she'd disappeared in that black bikini of hers. Rosy and pink. Blonde hair hangs down her shoulders, framing a face that is lit by a teasing smile. She knows exactly what she's doing, sitting topless opposite me like this.

It's revenge. She saw me looking yesterday, and now she's torturing me with it. Why did the damn woman insist on hating me like this?

You'd rather *she hated you,* my inner voice reminds me. *You can't disappoint her that way.*

"Your turn to start," she says. The warmth of her voice has dropped an octave.

Does she do this kind of thing often? I don't think so, not from what I've seen of her in the last few weeks. Crying over her brother's baby news and baking us brownies and talking to staff like they're her best friends in the whole damn world.

I exchange one of my cards, doing my damnedest to focus. Things are going to get very obvious if I have to take off my now too-tight pants.

"You *are* allowed to look at me, you know," she murmurs. "It's difficult to play otherwise."

"I know that," I say testily, but my eyes immediately linger at her invitation. She's gloriously beautiful in the dim lighting. Everything about her is golden, even her smile, though it's rare to see it so in my company.

"Why isn't André here?" I ask. "I doubt he'd approve."

"And do I need a man's approval to sit here with you?" She exchanges one of her own cards before dealing out the river. I scarcely notice the cards being revealed.

"Of course you don't."

"I could ask you the same, you know. Why isn't one of your money-grabbing sidekicks here?"

"Sidekicks?"

"I don't want to call them anything degrading," she says, though the frown at the edge of her lips says quite the opposite. So she's noticed the women I've spent time with over the years then, not that she's often had the opportunity to.

Good. I know exactly who she's dated—a string of millionaires' sons and heirs. Boys with names like Trip and Archer. Polished sons of bitches with pedigree dripping from their pores. The kind of men Cole Porter *should* be friends with.

"Why do you care who I'd bring?"

"Why do you care about André?"

I reveal my cards across the table. Somehow, I'd managed to pull a flush out of my ass despite the temptation on display, addling my concentration.

She reveals her own lesser hand. "Whoops."

And damn if I don't feel victorious when she stands up and reaches for the zipper in her skirt. She gives a light shake of her hips to wiggle out of it and her breasts bounce and *holy hell* I'm screwed.

The fabric falls gently to the floor around her ankles. Firelight dances across her body, covered in nothing but a pair of thin, lacy panties the color of her skin. This time, I don't pretend to avert my eyes. I drink her in instead.

There's victory in her eyes, too, when she sees my gaze. "I think we've changed the motives for this game," I say thickly.

"Have we?"

"Clearly, this was never about forgiveness for that poker game years ago." I reach for the cards and try not to focus on the length of her bare legs stretched out on the couch in front of me.

"Perhaps not," she admits. "Perhaps it was about something else entirely."

I deal us five cards each. She wants me to admit it, admit to the want she'd seen in me yesterday—that she's no doubt seeing on my face now. But if she thinks she can break me, she's just proven how little she knows me.

My hand comes down flat on the table. "I'm not a man who plays games, Blair."

"Except poker," she says calmly, as if she's not practically naked before me. I refuse to believe she's that unaffected. Let her see it, then—let her see what fire she's playing with.

Looking at my cards, I have two queens. It's too good a hand for what I need to happen. Watching her make similar calculations, I exchange one of my queens for a four. When the river has been laid and we reveal our hands, she wins by quite a margin.

"I thought you were good at poker," she demures.

I rise to my feet and look down at her as I undo the belt and zipper of my pants. How easy it would be to imagine a different scenario. Her dressed just like that, but on her knees in front of me.

Focus, man.

"Perhaps I'm used to less distracting opponents." I push down my trousers roughly, kicking them off. The relief of more space is nothing compared to the widening of her eyes as she sees the bulge in my boxers.

And fuck if it doesn't twitch at her gaze.

"Well," she says, and then says nothing more. I allow myself a crooked smile. She might talk a big game, but in the end, she is nowhere near in control of this.

I take a seat on the couch as if my raging hard-on is nothing more than a nuisance. "Your turn to deal," I say.

She nods and reaches for the cards. Shuffling in silence, there's a flush rising on her cheeks that I'd bet good money isn't from the wine or the heat of the fire.

"We're matched now," she says finally.

"Indeed we are." I turn up two of the cards she's dealt me. With a one-pair, winning isn't impossible. The idea of her skimming out of her panties... fuck. Forcing my mind to think through the fog, I ask, "do you ever think things through?"

Her eyes snap to mine. "Of course I do."

"Really," I say, pitching my tone to hurt. It's the only emotion I know I can reliably call forward. "And where is this little game supposed to lead, huh?"

Her exhale is shaky, but the fire burning in her eyes is fierce. My angry kitten, indeed. "To victory, of course."

"Ah." I exchange one of my cards for the river and secure another nine. A triple, now. There's no way I'm *not* winning. "And after this, you'll stop holding the poker game from eight years ago over my head?"

"Yes." She deals the river, eyes studying the cards. Her hair falls forward. Would it feel like golden silk through my fingers?

She reveals her three-pair of sevens. There's a smile on her lips.

I reveal my nines. "Damn," I say softly. "I guess you're not playing for victory at all."

Blair stands, her breasts rising and falling with the depth of her sigh. "Perhaps I'm not aiming for *that* kind of victory," she says darkly, reaching for her panties.

And that's when her words sink in. She'd consider this a victory—me, watching her. Me, aroused by her. Her dislike is still there, coloring her words and her perception of me. This has never been about starting something—only confirming it. And letting her know I want her would be losing.

"*No.*" My order is whip-like. "Those stay on."

"But I lost." Her fingers curl around the lacy fabric on her hips, ready to tug them down. "Are you saying it would be too much? Too difficult to... I don't know... control ourselves?"

I turn from her, from the softness of her skin and the curves of her body. My blood is pounding in my ears. The line between what I can have and what I want has never been this clearly marked before.

There is no path to victory here. In her direction lies only failure. What I can offer her won't be enough. Not to mention ruining *this* will ruin my friendship with Cole as well. It's too high a price.

So I say the one thing that I know she'll hate hearing, pitching my voice to nastiness. "Perhaps I don't *want* to see any more."

The silence in her direction tells me I've hit home, at least enough to stop the stripping. Thank God for the small mercies, I think, as I turn back and see those panties still in place.

But the expression on her face isn't the hurt I'd expected. It's something far worse. *Speculation.*

"Fine," she says. "I'll keep them on. Who knew Nicholas Park was a prude?" And then, as calmly as if she were fully dressed, she starts gathering up the cards.

I stare at her for longer than I should, want and anger chasing one another through my veins. And despite it all, a begrudging respect. She had seen me looking yesterday and all but confirmed my attraction today.

"You won, then." She shuffles them one last time before

heading to the dresser to put the cards back. As she bends over, I'm greeted with one of the best views of my life.

Yeah, I need to get out of here. Right now.

"At least there's that," I say, edging backwards. "Good night, Blair."

If she says it back, it's not something I hear. I'm already halfway down the hallway to my bedroom, my hand itching to wrap itself around the steel ache she'd inspired.

Blair Porter just got a whole new level of dangerous.

———

The next day is a very delicious kind of torture. Forced to meet her gaze at breakfast, knowing how her breasts look beneath her soft sweater. Seeing her long legs in ski pants, knowing how soft her thighs appear. Blair might have confirmed something for herself, but she had ignited the desire in me that I'd managed to keep at bay for years.

It's made worse when Cole comments on it. "You all right, man? You've been quiet all morning."

I hand him the gear we'll need for the glacier tour and refuse to look in Blair's direction, to see the humor I suspect is in her eyes at the question. "I'm fine."

Cole drops it, knowing when not to push, and sits beside me in the car. A friend when I've had none, Cole is better than I deserve. The episode last night made that especially clear—what would he say if he knew I'd let his sister undress in front of me?

I banish the thought, just like I have with so many others, focusing on the tour instead. The magnificent landscapes of frozen ice are enough to make my thoughts seem insignificant in comparison.

Blair seems to think the same thing. In the ice cave, she sidles up to me, her cheeks flushed by the biting cold. "Look," she says, pointing. "Is that an ice waterfall?"

"Looks like it." A forty-foot drop of sheer blue ice, diving straight into the glacier.

"Isn't it gorgeous?" The joy in her gold-brown eyes isn't faked, nor is the sincerity of her smile. She's radiant.

"Yes," I say quietly. "It is." And just as painfully out of my reach as it's always been, and a game of strip poker had done nothing to change that.

It had only confirmed it.

9

BLAIR

Leaves that have long since fallen are crusty with frost under my boots as I walk down the city street. The season is changing, and it's changing fast, bringing with it the same nip in the air that we had up in Whistler the past weekend. A few of the window display I pass have already begun hanging their Christmas decorations.

I tuck my scarf in more tightly around my neck and try not to dwell on the memory. Whatever happened, happened. The only thing I can do now is to be professional—to follow to the letter the agreement we'd made. Civility and profit.

Besides, what had my strip poker escapade changed, really? Nothing—except that I know for a fact Nick is attracted to me. It felt like a victory at the time, to see that he wasn't as aloof as he'd always seemed. After nearly a decade of admiring him from afar, the realization had been overwhelming.

But in the days since, it's become a hollow victory. So he's a man who responds to a half-naked woman. *How rare.*

It doesn't matter if he's attracted to me—he made it clear he's not going to act on it—and he still doesn't *like* me. The only person he ever smiles at or shares a laugh with is my brother.

I push open the door to the innocuous brick building that houses his capital venture firm. No sign, no valet, no lobby. It's exactly the kind of no-bullshit person he's always been. *I'm not a man who plays games, Blair.*

Gina greets me by the door. Her usually calm composure seems frayed, her eyes showing relief when I show up. When has that ever been the case?

"Is everything all right?"

"Yes and no," she says. "I can't accompany Mr. Park to the warehouse visit today. I've just informed him about it as well."

I put my bag down on the nearby desk. "Why not? What's wrong?"

"Family emergency. Nothing bad," she adds, seeing my gaze. "But frustrating. I have to take care of it. It's bad timing, that's all."

"Whatever you have to do," I say. "I can reschedule the visit for you, if you'd like."

"No, no rescheduling. There's not enough time as there is, and we need to implement the changes for the store. Can you go in my stead?"

My world spins, but only for a moment. Gina is entrusting me with this. "Absolutely. If you have the time, give me a rundown of what you'd planned to do today, and I'll take it from there."

Relief shines in her otherwise professional-to-a-fault expression. She nods, her bobbed hair dipping with the movement. "Let's begin, then. I've already informed Mr. Park that you'll take my place today."

I ignore the knotting of nerves in my stomach. "Thank you. These are the binders you prepared?"

"Yes, they have your suggestions for logo designs and store layouts in them. Now… this is the itinerary I'd drawn up." She pauses, looking over at me appraisingly. "I know you two are family friends. But when he's at work like this, he doesn't want to waste time. Briefing him on the planned changes should be efficient and focused."

I nod. Her tone steadies me. There are guidelines to this. *Profit and civility.* Twenty minutes later, I'm knocking on the door to Nick's office, my bag slung over my shoulder and the binders tucked under my arm.

He opens the door himself. Towering before me, his dark eyes are guarded. "Good. You're finished. Let's go."

He strides past me through the office and I hurry to catch up, cursing myself for choosing to wear booties with heels. I'd dressed for a quiet day at the office, not a field trip.

Nick holds the front door open for me and we walk side by side to the parking garage next door. I try to ignore the thrill that his nearness brings, that it always brings, especially when he's suit-clad like this.

The fact that we haven't spoken a word alone to one another since the poker game hasn't helped.

We've seen each other half-naked.

That fact hangs in the air, unacknowledged and undiscussed, a steady presence. It's there when he unlocks his Land Rover without another glance at me. It hovers between us as I slide into the passenger seat.

He pulls out into the central Seattle traffic. I've never seen him drive, and despite the odd mood between us, my eyes stray to his hands on the wheel. The backs of his hands are wide. Knuckles broad. Tan, slightly rough skin.

His displeasure is heavy. *That makes two of us,* I think. There would have been no awkwardness with Gina here. How are we to survive the one-hour drive?

I break the quiet fifteen minutes in. He might be perfectly content with pressured silence, but I'm not.

"You don't have a driver," I note. My brother had had one for a long time, treasuring the time it saved him—most of his texts and calls were handled from the back of a car.

"Astute observation," Nick says. His tone is just the way he likes it: dismissive and mean, all rolled into one.

I glance out the window. "I was just comparing it to Cole."

He's quiet for a beat. "I'm not dependent on anyone," he says. "Cole is right about it being a time-saver. But you have to trust a driver."

And I don't trust anyone. He doesn't say the words, but my mind speaks them for him regardless.

"You trust a pilot to fly a plane," I point out. "You trusted the pilot up in Whistler on the helicopter ride."

"I can't fly a plane or a helicopter myself," he says. Are the words spoken through gritted teeth? I bite my lip to hide a smile.

"So you only trust people when you have no other choice."

He shakes his head. In profile, the rough cut of his jaw stands out sharply, as does the dark stubble on his cheeks and jaw. "You're impossible."

"But correct?"

"Potentially." In the silence that follows, his voice softens, but it's not with kindness. "I trust you won't say anything about our game in Whistler."

I cross my arms. "Do you think I would?"

"I don't know."

"If you're worried about Cole, don't be. I'm not in the habit of telling my brother when I get undressed with a man." I pull open one of the binders at random, opening it in my lap. "Let's focus on the day instead. Do you know who we're going to meet?"

I don't let him answer. I dive into an explanation instead, preparing him in short, concise sentences. *Be Gina,* I tell myself. If Nick wants to kill whatever attraction exists between us with professionalism, well, two can play that game.

We arrive at the store with time to spare. Pulling into the backlot, he reaches for his phone. "They might not like us here," he warns me.

I frown at him. I'd had email contact with the head of this warehouse. She had been nothing but accommodating.

"Why wouldn't they?"

"They have a hiring freeze, same as all the others," he tells me. "They will have been working double shifts. They know bankruptcy is looming."

A response blooms on my tongue but dies as it reaches my lips. *But we're here to save the store.* That might be my intent, but I

73

know it's not Nick's, not really. The endgame for him is profit. If it's by saving the brand or by eventually selling the individual stores and supply chains to the highest bidder, it's all the same to him.

Nick turns, as if he's read this and more in my eyes. I follow him into the warehouse with steel in my spine. If he expects me to fail, I won't. The binder Gina's prepared?

I'd written most of the content.

———

Nick and I emerge nearly an hour and a half later in tense silence. I'd kept my sentences short, but civil, and straight to the point—not an extraneous word.

He didn't comment much, either, apart from a few questions here and there. We've been civil to the point of rudeness, and as we get back into the car, the tension between us has in no way lessened.

We're halfway to Seattle, deafening silence reigning, when the car begins to slow. I look over at Nick. Has he forgotten where the gas pedal is?

He steers to the side and turns on the warning light of the car. "Damn."

"What's happening?"

"Must have blown a tire."

I turn around to check, but there's no one behind us. The road is empty in both directions and nothing surrounds us but trees, pines standing tall and straight. I step out into the cold.

"Do you have a spare?"

"Of course I do."

I wrap my jacket tighter around myself and start inspecting the tires on my side. My mood sours even further, but I refuse to let it show in my face or in my tone. Let him be the one stuck in a constant bad mood.

Watch me be civil.

"It's this one," I call out, seeing the small rubber tear. How had I not felt it when it happened?

"Damn." Nick runs a hand over his head, across the short crop of his midnight-black hair. "Stay in the car while I change it."

The order is barked. It's clearly not for my benefit—I bet he just wants me out of the way.

"I can help," I offer, anything to get us moving faster. I've never changed a tire before, nor seen anyone do it. But I have two hands and I'm willing to use them.

He speaks from the trunk of the car. "Oh, I doubt that very much."

The words slice through me. I'm tired of this. Hadn't we made progress this past weekend? "Why are you rude to me? We agreed to civility."

He doesn't respond. The only sound I hear is that of him unfolding something in the back, pulling at plastic and rubber.

I walk around the car to face him. "For me, the reason was the old poker game, and we settled that. But what's your excuse, huh?"

He lifts the heavy tire effortlessly, his arms straining against the fabric of his suit. "Why do I have to like you in order to work with you? Is it necessary?"

"Of course not. I just thought—"

"Thought what? That because I find you beautiful I somehow *like* you, too? Plenty of women are attractive." The fierceness in his voice burns, humiliation creeping up my cheeks. I feel like I did all those years ago—dismissed.

He shakes his head, as if he's disgusted by our interaction, and begins changing the tire with furious movements.

I stare at him for a long moment.

And then I take a seat in the passenger seat, slamming the door behind me. We don't speak a word the entire way back to the city.

10

BLAIR

My brother's house has been transformed. The event organizers have gone all out, with string lights around the wrap-around porch. The marble floor in the entry is polished to a shine and drink tables line the walls. Rooms on the second floor are locked and closed off, and below, staff filters in and out of the house in preparation.

Skye comes to stand next to me as we watch cars slowly roll up the long driveway. She's barely started to show, and in the dress she's wearing, the faint bump of her stomach is well-hidden.

"Right," she says quietly. "And so it begins."

"Do you feel ready?"

"To play hostess? I've learned a thing or two over the past year." She leans against me, our shoulders touching. "Your brother hosts more than his share of events."

I smile crookedly. Cole has a fine appreciation for parties like this—for the networking opportunities they present. He knows that he can extend an invitation to the right people and most would come on the basis of his reputation alone. A smile here and a handshake there and he paves the way for future business ventures.

In many ways, I want to be like him. It's that quiet desire that once drove me to start my own fashion brand. Watching the cars being carefully parked by the hired valets, I let my mind trace the contours of that old failure again.

For a long time, I hadn't wanted to be seen in public. The headlines had been that scathing. *Unfinished and unformed,* they'd called my collection. *Derivative.* One reviewer had written a sentence that made my heart stop. *She's clearly wasting her brother's money, but then again, he has money to waste.*

I had prayed for Cole to never read that article. But it little mattered if he did—the truth had been there anyway. Not that he had ever once breathed a word of that sentiment to me.

"Ah," Skye sighs, a sound of relief, as Cole heads toward us. Taking the porch steps in two and with his form-fitting suit, he looks every inch the rich asshole media likes to portray him as. Something in Skye relaxes as my brother puts an arm around her waist.

"Are you ready, ladies?" He'd prepped us on the game plan before—which individuals he most needed a word alone with.

I paste a charming smile on my face. If there's one thing I'm confident in, it's my ability to conquer a party. "I'm *always* ready to mingle."

"If only it were an Olympic sport," Cole teases. "You'd be a gold medalist."

"I'm sure you could make that a thing. Perhaps for my birthday?"

And then it's showtime as the first guests walk up the steps. I shake hands and pad egos and welcome people inside, doing my best to turn on the dazzle.

I'd really indulged in the preparations for tonight. My wrap dress is deep green, accentuating my curves, and I'd made sure my hair was blow-dried bouncy and smooth. In my head, I'd been doing all of this for my brother—for his party, his investors, to better play my part.

But the face I'd seen in my mind's eye had been Nick's. His angry words still ring in my head, but with a day to think it over, I'm not humiliated by them anymore.

I'm angry, too.

He'd be at this party, that much I'm certain of, but I can't seem to spot him. I find someone else instead.

Or more accurately perhaps, someone else finds me. "Blair Porter," a young man says warmly, leaning in for a practiced kiss on my cheek. It's a forward greeting, but I find myself smiling back at him instinctually. "I'm Bryce Adams. It's lovely to finally meet you—Maddie mentions you nonstop."

Then the realization pierces through. *Bryce Adams,* of B.C. Adams. He's here, and so is Nick. Why on earth would Cole have invited him?

My smile doesn't falter, though my eyes dart up behind him to scan the room. "Likewise—I've heard good things. I met your father, I believe, a month back?"

"Yes, he told me. He was quite impressed, you know." His brown hair falls playfully over his brow and he reaches up to push it back.

"How have you been?"

"Well, you know how things are." He gives me a pained smile. "I'm finding myself at a loss for what to do, now that my future calling is no longer in the picture."

There's a stab of unexpected guilt in my stomach. Coming face-to-face with the man whose family legacy I'm helping to dismantle...

I reach out and put a hand on his arm. "I'm sorry. I can't begin to understand how that must feel."

"Thank you," he says, putting a hand over mine on his arm, stopping me from pulling back. "The worst is hearing how our employees are faring. All the shutdowns and firings. The people we've let down by selling."

It twists right at the heart of my own concerns. Despite that, I can't let him disparage Nick quite like that.

"You did what you had to do," I say. "Just as the new owners are doing."

Bryce opens his mouth to reply but there's no sound. His

blue gaze catches on something behind me instead, growing steely with resolve. *Oh no.*

He brushes past me with a quiet *excuse me* and strides toward the one person I've been looking for all night and haven't been able to find.

Nick turns just in time. In the dim light and against his dark suit, his eyes look pitch-black. There's no hint of surprise or fear on his face as he takes in Bryce, stopping before him.

Bryce's voice vibrates with rage. "You looked my grandfather in the eye and told him you'd take care of his employees. That's the only reason he agreed to sell to you. And now you've laid off more than two hundred of them. How do you get up in the morning?"

"I usually set an alarm," Nick replies, his voice arctic.

"That's what you have to say for yourself?"

"Your grandfather knew who he sold his company to," Nick says. "And if he cared so much about his employees, he wouldn't have driven the business to within an inch of its life." If Bryce is angry, Nick is fury itself, cold and controlled and carefully leashed.

I'm dimly aware of people watching the interaction. Of conversations hushed and eyes following. Bryce's right arm twitches. He's an inch from blows, I realize, my eyes flitting to Nick's.

But Nick has already made the same realization. He widens his stance, growing impossibly taller. "I made your family a good offer. You'll be wealthy for the rest of your life, despite your abject business failure. Consider yourself lucky."

His words drip with dismissal. Bryce glances about, his eyes incredulous. *Are you hearing this?*

And people are.

Bryce steps closer. "We should never have agreed to your deal. I might not have the company anymore, nor a vote on the board, but people still know our name. We can cause a lot of trouble for you."

"Go ahead and try."

Bryce shakes his head in disgust. "You can put on a suit all you like, but you're no less trash for that."

Nick's eyes flash. For a wild second, I think he might actually punch Bryce. The violent tension in the air is flavored by the crowd's horrified delight.

I take a step forward, not knowing what to do but needing to do *something*.

Nick sees me. Impassivity returns to his features, the fire in his eyes gone as quick as it had come. "I'd suggest you accept your fate gracefully," he counsels Bryce, condescension in his tone.

And then he walks away, taking a sip of his brandy and ignoring the looks the entire room shoots his way. If they burn like arrows in his back, he doesn't show it, standing straight and proud.

Bryce is panting like he's run a race. I step forward, placing a hand with more gentleness on his arm than I feel. The bastard must have come here uninvited with the sole intent of confronting Nick.

"Come on," I tell him, guiding him out of the living room. He lets me, eyes still furious.

"Can you believe him?" he mutters, as if he's forgotten who he's talking to. Nick and Cole's friendship is well-documented.

"I can." My voice is curt.

No one bothers us as we make our way out through the front door. I lift a hand for one of the waiting cabs, but Bryce barely notices me, he's so lost in his own thoughts.

"Bryce, I think it's time you head out," I say.

His gaze finds mine. "Yes. But—no, you're right." He looks over his shoulder. "This is your brother's party. I'm sorry for making a scene like that."

"It's all right," I say, though I truly don't feel like it is. "But in the future, if you have any grievances with Nick, you should take them to his office. Not in a place like this."

Bryce's self-assured smile is back in place. It's tinged with bashfulness, his eyes pleading on mine. "You're right. Can you ever forgive me?"

The nerve of the man, to flirt like this when he's just... "I'll think about it," I say.

He meets my serious tone with playfulness. "I'll be waiting."

Behind him, my brother bursts through the door. The scowl on his face is familiar. If he comes out now, he'll ruin my attempt at getting Bryce out without making *more* of a scene.

I give him a quiet shake of the head and watch as he reins himself in. I know he hates every second of it.

Bryce gets into the cab I've hailed with a final glance at me. "Goodbye, Blair," he tells me. There's speculation in his gaze and damn it, I should have told him I work for Nick. That would have put an end to *that* real quick.

"I didn't invite him," Cole says darkly by my side. "How he got past the event planners, I have no idea."

"He's a smooth talker."

"Did you hear the argument?"

I sigh. "Yes. Nick took him down verbally, but everyone heard."

"Damn." The annoyance on his face lasts only a few moments before it clears, and he's once again my composed big brother, ready to conquer and charm. "I'll have to apologize to Nick later. If he'll even accept it, that is. Perhaps he enjoyed it."

I match his pace as we walk back through the house. Enjoyed the confrontation... Somehow, I doubt that. "I'll check on him," I say quietly. "I think you should reduce tensions in the living room. People are bound to gossip."

Cole raises his eyebrow but doesn't comment. "I will."

And then I'm off again, trying to adopt the same breezy manner I'd had before, but finding that it's slipped out of my grasp all together.

Nick's not in any of the major party areas. He's not outside, with the smokers, or together with the crowd around the hors d'oeuvres. He's nowhere at all.

I pause with my foot on the staircase. The second story is off-limits for guests tonight. Both staff and security are on sight to help stop that. Glancing around, I give one of the security guards a smile more confident than I feel. *Please, Cole, tell me you put me on the OK-list...*

The guard gives a curt nod. I dart upstairs, and in the darkness, begin my search, checking each door.

Bingo—he's in Cole's study.

Standing on the balcony with his back to me, a glass of brandy dangling from his fingers, Nick doesn't turn when I enter.

My heart is beating fast. For a wild second, I feel like I'm approaching a cornered animal. An absurd image of me holding out my hands, palms up, and saying *calm, boy* flits through my mind.

I clear my throat, but Nick speaks first. "I wondered if you'd come searching for me."

From the scathing tone, it's clear that's not a good thing. I swallow again. "Bryce wasn't invited. Cole doesn't know how he got in."

"I pity the security he hired, then." There's dark humor in Nick's tone at the thought, but when he speaks again, it's gone. "So? Have you come to tell me you agree with everything Bryce said?"

"No," I say. "No, not at all."

He turns around, dark eyes in the dimly lit room. "He only said what you've been thinking about all along, especially in regard to the layoffs."

"He was spiteful and bitter. He wasn't speaking truthfully at all."

Nick rolls his eyes. "He was bitter, yes. *And* truthful. Come now, surely he said nothing you haven't already thought yourself."

His black mood gives rise to my own. Whatever he's goading me to say, I won't give it to him. "I made sure he left as quickly as possible. Cole is down there now, trying to stop gossip."

"Too late for that," he says. "This will only add to my reputation. Good for business, that."

I cross my arms across my chest. "I don't believe it."

"Believe what?"

"This act. You put it on all the time—just like the other day. Why?"

"Oh, Blair," he says, but it's not in a nice way. It's in a you-know-so-little way. "Why did you help me deal with Bryce?"

"What, is it so hard to believe I just *wanted* to?"

"You're helpful, yes, but that's not why you did it." He takes a step closer, a muscle working in his jaw. Almost absently, he puts down his brandy on Cole's desk. "Explain yourself."

"Is it impossible to believe that I disagreed with Bryce, that I'm actually starting to see merit in your work?"

He dismisses my words like they're obvious untruths. "It's your brother's party. Of course you don't want a scene. You'd do anything for him and Skye."

His words fan the flames of my irritation and they lick my insides with fire. "Why are you so determined to think everyone hates you? So intent on driving them away, to live up to the very worst of your reputation? To push and push until people give up?"

The fiery look on his features is new to me. There's nothing impassive about it, nothing cold or controlled. He steps closer. "Why do you keep trying with me? You give me chance after chance after chance, always hoping I'll redeem myself."

I throw my hands up. "I wish I knew!" I say. "But don't worry, I get it now. You don't want anyone to care about you except Cole, so you just push them away. Well, forgive me, because I did. I overstepped your arbitrary boundaries by actually giving—"

And then my words die on my lips because he's kissing them. The surprise lasts only a second under his warmth, and then I'm kissing him too, our lips moving together.

It's not a perfect kiss at first. It's rough and surprised and we don't quite fit and then we just *do*, like a key finally turning in a lock. His hands come around my waist as he tugs my body tightly against his. My lips open and he takes advantage of that and I'm not thinking any more, not at all.

I'm drowning in sensation. He's everywhere, from thigh to chest, rock solid and big and so much *more* than I'd imagined. There's no way to come back unscathed from this kiss. There will be a Blair *before* kissing Nick and a Blair *after* kissing Nick, altered forever by this experience.

I wrap my arms tightly around his neck. My nails rake gently through his dark hair and he groans, low in his throat. His hands flatten against my low back.

His tongue sweeps across my lower lip. Perhaps it's the brandy, or just him, but it sets fire to my mouth. I kiss him fiercely to stop the burn.

It only makes it grow hotter.

Somewhere far away, in some distant awareness, I register that Nick is moving us. That I'm stepping backwards, but I'm holding on to him and things like *tripping* or *furniture* seem inconsequential.

His hands drift lower to my thighs and then I'm lifted up, placed on some hard surface that gives me more access to him. I revel in it, running my hands over the wide stretches of his shoulders, feeling the thrumming of life inside his powerful frame. *Mine*, I think fiercely.

His hands grip my waist hard, and not once has he stopped kissing me. My legs open instinctively for him and he steps between them. Eager, I lift one up, hooking it around his hip. Nick growls against my lips at the movement.

When he tears his lips from mine, I barely have time to protest before he's put them back again, this time on my neck. A hand gently tugging in my hair tips my head back to give him more access. I stare unseeing up at the ceiling and hold on to his shoulders as sensations course through me. His lips against the hollow at the base of my throat spark me back into action.

And then I'm tugging at the buttons of his shirt. I need access to his skin too—it's not fair he's so much more covered up than me.

Nick glances down at my hands and then further down still, where his own are smoothing across my thighs. His fingers grip the green fabric of my wrap dress and toss it back impatiently, revealing the length of my bare thigh and just a hint of underwear.

"Yes," I murmur, moving to the edge of the desk, unaware of anything but him and this and us and *please just touch me.*

Nick takes a step back. The loss of his strong arms is so sudden that I have to slide off the desk to keep from tipping over.

The long, deep look we exchange infuriates me. How dare he look at me with so much want it's practically dripping from him and *not* touch me? Can't he see I'm burning?

I take a step forward but Nick backs away, reaching up to refasten the single button I'd managed to undo.

And right before my eyes, the raw need on his features dissipates, like ripples on a lake. He's once more the scathing, infuriating, cold-hearted man he pretends to be. Because I'm sure of that now. It's nothing but an act.

He opens his mouth to speak but seems to think better of it. In the next moment, he's gone, striding out the door and wrenching it open.

"Nick, don't—"

It's no use. He's vanished, and I'm left standing in the study, my heart pounding like I've just been sprinting flat-out and still lost the race.

11

BLAIR

The numbers bleed together on the screen. Every time I go over purchasing orders, I see Nick's eyes instead. And when I reach for fabric samples, the memory of his lips on mine threatens to overwhelm me. Nick had kissed me.

After nearly a decade of admiring him from afar, the experience has been overwhelming. Sure, he might still think of me as Cole's spoiled little sister, or as a socialite in need of a hobby, but he also kissed me like he needed me more than he needed air—and there was no way he could deny that.

We haven't spoken since. No, in the six days that have passed, he hasn't been around at all. Not at work, where he's either out with investors or taking meetings, and not at Cole's, where I'd been invited for dinner one evening.

He's avoiding me.

After walking out like that without a word, he seems intent on not giving me another. I'd chalked it up to Nick being Nick at first. To the words we've spoken before—my hasty assertion that he wants to push the world away—and not the kiss itself.

But as Thursday becomes Friday, and Friday bleeds into the weekend, his silence starts to grate on my self-confidence. It *had* been an absolutely unreal kiss, hadn't it?

On Saturday morning, I pack up a box of samples for my new

company and ignore the churning of nerves in my stomach. First Nick, and now this, all in the span of a week. *Be brave, Blair.*

The route to my brother's house in Greenwood Hills has become so familiar to me now that I could probably drive it blindfolded. Cole isn't in when I enter, but that matters little. It's his wife I'm here to see.

"Skye?"

"I'm upstairs!" she calls, and I hurry up the steps, my bag slung over my shoulder. Filled with all my hard work and plans and hopes, it feels far heavier than its actual weight.

"Where?"

"Over here!"

I find her in the room adjoining the master, sitting cross-legged on the floor. Her small stomach is really starting to show now, despite the flowy dress.

"I don't have any maternity clothes," she says sheepishly when she sees me looking. "So I'm wearing a summer dress in fall. Whoops."

"We can go shopping," I suggest, the idea momentarily cheering me up. "There are great maternity options, you know."

Skye's eyes lighten. "Do you want to play personal stylist again?"

"Is it that obvious?"

"Yes," she laughs, reaching over to put a hand on my knee. She tugs me down to the floor beside her. "But I don't mind. You know what I like."

Excitement floods to my lips before I can stop it. "Oh, we'll have so much fun. I already have a ton of ideas... maybe we can go tomorrow."

"We have time," Skye says, putting a hand over her stomach. "Months of it, in fact."

"Why are you in here?" I look around at the empty room, my hand fisting in the plush fabric of the carpet. "Oh! The nursery?"

She nods. "I've been sitting here looking at paint samples and ideas and trying to figure out how I want it to look."

"Will you show me?" My niece or nephew will sleep in this

87

room. It's easy to picture a little girl or boy with Cole and Skye's dark hair, grinning just like my brother over the bars of her crib.

"Yes, but first, will you tell me what's in your bag? Are you planning on moving in?"

I laugh, but it's a bit high-pitched. Pulling my bag into the space between us, I pause with my hands on the zipper. *Courage.*

"So… I've been keeping a little secret."

Skye's eyes widen in mock horror. "I can't help you bury a body."

I laugh, a bit of tension draining off. It's just Skye, after all. "Ouch, but no, that's not what I'm asking. I've been working on something and I want your feedback." With more composure than I feel, I unzip the bag and start pulling out samples.

One by one, I lay them out beside us. A silky slip. A nude-colored bra. Seamless underwear, all packaged in little silken bags. A pair of Spanx-like shorts. A negligee, made from the same silk mix as the slip.

"What's this?" Skye carefully reaches out to touch the soft material. "These are gorgeous."

"They're all my design," I say. "Instead of a fashion line, I've been working on a brand that supplies undergarments and fashion… solutions, I guess I'd call them, like fashion tape. Everything you need to make your already existing wardrobe work better, but sold together under one brand."

Skye is lifting up the slip, looking at the lace. "This is gorgeous. The finishing…"

I nod, excited now, my words spilling fast. "It took me forever to find the perfect fabric, and then the right maker. I want it to be the best quality—they'll last forever."

"When have you had time to do this?"

"I've had nothing but time until I started working for Nick," I say. It's liberating to finally admit it.

"When are you going to launch?"

"Not yet. I want to think this through," I say. "I want it to launch as a coherent brand, with a web presence, and online store, all of it."

"Cole would love—"

"No," I say immediately. "Cole can't know. Not yet."

Skye's face drops. "Blair, he'd be nothing but supportive."

Guilt twists my insides. "Oh, I know that, trust me. But..." And here it is, the thing I don't want to say. He would offer to invest, just like he had with my previous fashion line, which had failed so catastrophically.

Or even worse—he *wouldn't* offer, and I'd know that he didn't believe in me anymore. I wouldn't give him the choice until I had something working that was up and running.

"This needs to be mine," I say finally, thinking of all my own money I'm sinking into this. "I want to prove it to myself. That I can do it on my own."

Skye nods slowly. "I can understand that," she says, reaching over for one of the bras. "You really designed these? They're gorgeous."

"Thank you. That's one of the slogans I'm workshopping, actually. *Making practicality pretty.* The pieces I brought are all for your skin tone. Would you mind very much testing them out? Wear them sometimes in the coming weeks? I need feedback."

Skye nods, a hand back on her stomach. "Of course, yes. I'd love to, for as long as I can."

She's the first person I've ever told about this. It's been over a year of working from home, of ordering samples and creating website layouts and running the numbers, and now it's here. "Thank you," I say.

Maybe she hears my sincerity, or maybe it's just the kind of person she is, but she puts her hand on mine. "Anytime. We're family now, you know, *Aunt.*"

I laugh. "I don't know if I'll ever get used to that."

"You'll have to. God, I'll be called *Mom* soon." Skye shakes her head in wonder at the thought. "I'm still in disbelief."

"And you'll be a great one." I glance over my shoulder, grateful for my brother's prolonged absence. "Where's Dad-to-be today?"

"He's trying out our new tennis court with Nick," she says.

He's here? My muscles lock in place at the notion. So somewhere in their massive garden, Nick is sweating and swatting tennis balls and *still* avoiding me.

The words slip out before I can stop them. "I didn't know he'd be here."

Skye's eyes flare with interest. "Has something happened between you two?"

"No," I lie. "It's just… you know we don't get along. And working together has already stretched all the patience I have."

There's a furrow between Skye's eyebrows. "Well, something seemed off with him. You've known him longer, but… don't you think a proper relationship would be good for him?"

I want to laugh and cry at the same time. I settle for a dark chuckle. "I'm sure it would be, were he interested in having one."

"You think he's not?"

"Skye, he's not been in one for as long as I've known him," I say honestly. "I think he likes his solitude."

After the confrontation we'd had just a few days ago—in a study down the hall, no less—I didn't doubt that at all. Keeping people at arm's length is probably his method of living, as ingrained in him as the need to breathe.

"Well, no man was made to live alone," Skye says decisively, rising from the floor. "Do you want a cup of tea? We can look at paint samples and I can pick your brain."

Glad she's dropped the Nick conversation, I give her a beaming smile. "As a nursery expert, I'm at your service."

Skye rolls her eyes at me but leads the way back down to the kitchen. I lean against the giant island and watch her prepare two cups. Despite myself, I keep glancing at the back door. My earlier peace and calm is shattered.

He's here somewhere.

She hands me a cup. "Thank you," I murmur, using the spoon to stir.

"So, these are the ones I'm thinking about…" She pulls out a binder of colors and we study them for a long while, our heads bent together.

We're startled by the back door opening, my brother and Nick falling in through it like they're eighteen rather than thirty. Nick doesn't keep Cole at an arm's-lengths distance, I note bitterly.

And then he sees me.

Nick straightens immediately. The sweat on his brow glistens, the material of the flimsy workout T-shirt clinging to his broad chest.

Cole sees us too, but he smiles. "Here to raid our fridge, Lairy?"

The old nickname does nothing for my already flushed cheeks. I roll my eyes at him. "That was *you*, years ago. My own is quite well-stocked, thank you very much."

"We've been looking at designs for the nursery," Skye says. "How was the new tennis court?"

"Excellent," Cole says. "So excellent, in fact, that I won."

Nick's upper lip lifts. "You had the home turf advantage. I won't go so easy next time."

I turn my eyes away from him. If I look too long, I'll remember, and if I remember, I'll drown in the memory.

Skye grabs her cup of tea and the binder with colors. "Come on, let me show you the paint swatches Blair and I decided on. The nursery is on the way to the shower anyway."

My brother pauses only for a second to nod at Nick. "The guest bath is yours."

Nick inclines his head. "Thanks."

And then Cole and Skye are gone, despite the fact that we hadn't decided on any paint swatches at all.

Sly dog, I think, wondering how much Skye suspects. How much she's guessed and pieced together. Her comment about Nick needing a relationship…

Nick runs a hand through his hair. For all his power and skill when he's in a suit, or the way he commands attention at a party, he's just a man now. One who's sweaty and flushed and alone here with me.

I take a step closer. "Avoiding me, are you?"

"Not at all."

"Really? Not being at your own office for five days straight seems... well, excessive."

"I've had out-of-office meetings. B.C. Adams isn't my only investment, you know." The fire in his eyes doesn't match the cool detachment in his voice.

I put my cup of tea down harder than planned. "So you're determined to pretend as if nothing happened?"

"*Nothing* did happen, Blair," he says through clenched teeth. As if he can will it to be true if he says it enough times. But I'm not like that.

"Coward," I toss at him.

Something clenches in his jaw. "See, this is why I didn't want to have this discussion."

"So you *were* avoiding me," I say triumphantly. "You know, it's not hard to say the right thing. You can take your pick. 'I'm not interested, Blair.' That's possible. Or, perhaps, 'I don't think it's a good idea, what with us working together.' Do you want me to write the script for you?"

He steps closer, the smell of Nick and man and faint sweat hitting me. There's not even a pretense of sophistication today—no suit or bowtie. It's all roughness.

"Does there have to be a *reason*?" he asks. "Isn't it enough that it's not a good idea? That your big brother is in the same goddamn house right now and that I'd rather not lose his friendship?"

I wet my lip. His eyes dart down, both of us moving despite ourselves. "You really think he'd mind?"

"Oh yes." Nick's voice is black and heavy with insinuation.

"Well, then," I murmur, "do we have to tell him?"

His hand reaches up and catches a strand of my hair between his fingers. My breath stops altogether, eyes locked on his. "Tell him what, exactly?"

"That we're getting to know one another better," I say. "After all, isn't that what he's always wanted?"

Nick's lips curl into a sardonic smile. The expression sets my heart into overdrive. "I'm not sure that's the way he intended."

"So?" Brave or foolish, I don't know, but I've lost the ability to control my actions. My arms wrap around his neck of their own accord, the warmth of his worked-up skin burning against mine. His hands come up around my waist—to push me away or pull me closer?

"You can't tell me you didn't enjoy kissing me," I murmur. "That much was obvious."

"Well," he says quietly. "I'd have to be dead not to enjoy that."

And then I'm pressing my lips against his, and he's groaning into my mouth, hands at my waist finally finding their resolve and pulling me closer. He's big and sweaty and I don't mind at all. If anything, it makes him feel even more overwhelmingly alive against me.

Nick kisses me back fiercely, the kisses every inch as powerful as the ones we'd shared in Cole's study. They burn—they brand.

He breaks away from my lips with a groaned curse. "Fuck. You'll be the death of me, Blair."

I'm breathing too hard to respond. He pushes me away firmly, shaking his head. "Not here," he growls. "Not *now.*"

The promise in his words makes my stomach tighten. Somewhere else, then. Some other time. I reach up to straighten my blouse, feigning more composure than I feel. Inside my chest, my heart is hammering.

We watch each other for a long moment. The smile on his face is gone now, replaced by an intensity I'm unused to. "I'm not sure you know what you're asking for," he says.

I look back at him levelly, thinking about the way he keeps people at a distance, at the words I'd spoken to him just last week. *I'm sorry for caring, all right?*

If someone would get hurt, it would be me. And yet… I find myself thinking that perhaps it would be worth it.

Steps echo down the hallway. With the grace of a large predator, Nick strides away from me, grabbing a discarded training bag from the floor. He disappears down the opposite hallway toward the guest bath before Skye returns to the kitchen.

She gives me an innocent smile. "All good here?" she asks.

I take a sip of my now-cold tea. "Yes," I say, forcing my voice even. "All good."

12

NICK

Never before had a woman's lips so haunted me. Logically, realistically, I know they're not different than others I've kissed. That what she'd been suggesting—*getting to know one another better*—was something I could find anywhere else. Why risk ruining everything by indulging in it with her?

And yet, my traitorous body wanted it more than it had ever wanted anything. Worse still was that my mind seemed committed to joining the mutiny. It circled back to focus on her more times than I could count. On wheat-blonde hair and honey-brown eyes. On the smile that always seemed to hover around the edges of her lips, ready to break through like the sun through clouds. Too beautiful for me—she was sincerity and laughter and goodness.

Was that why her lips affected me like no other woman's ever had? After our encounter in her brother's study at that godawful party, they had nearly brought me to my knees.

I shake my head at my own thoughts. Staying away is no longer an option. Minimizing fallout—that has to be my priority now. So I go to work the following Monday, not scheduling any out-of-office meetings, to show both her and I that we can handle it.

That I'm stronger than my attraction.

Blair's at work early. Bent over her desk in the open landscape, her hair is neatly curled down her back and a red, silken blouse curving around her form.

I stop by her desk. It's the first time I've visited her desk in these past weeks—or acknowledged her at all when not mediated by Gina. One by one, the firewalls I've erected seem to be coming down.

She pushes away the commissioned logo designs for B.C. Adams and looks up at me with surprise. "Mr. Park?"

Mr. Park. She only ever calls me that at work. I can only imagine how much she hates saying the words.

"I want an evening briefing tonight," I say. There are only a few other employees in the room, and they know better than to eavesdrop, but I make sure my voice is professional.

"Of course." Something about the softness of the words makes me want to smile. "Yes. Should I prepare anything?"

"No. I just want your opinions." Our gaze catches and holds, and there's a ton of questions in hers. "Be in my office by seven."

"Certainly." I can see the quiet confusion in her eyes, but after the way she'd ambushed me in her brother's kitchen... we'll have this conversation here, far away from prying eyes.

The rest of the day is packed, as usual, and yet I find it hard to focus on anything but her pending arrival. It's a relief when my assistant finally announces her arrival, a few minutes past seven.

She's late.

My brandy sends a familiar burn down my throat. Rare are the times when I drink in my office in the evenings—yet one more thing she's reduced me to doing.

"Hi," she says. Her hair falls like golden silk around her face. "I'm here."

"I can see that." I gesture for the chair opposite my desk.

She sits down, crossing her legs. "So?" she asks. "Am I here to be fired? Reprimanded? Told off for the other day?"

"Those are the only options you could think of?"

"Oh, I have about a hundred more on the list, but these seemed the most likely."

My lips curve. "None of those three, actually."

"Oh? You surprise me."

"My goal in life," I say, her eyes widening at the teasing. I haven't often indulged in that with her. "So you want to get to know one another better."

Blair's eyes blaze at my words. The fire there is one I'm used to seeing—but it's never before been turned on me in anything but irritation. The change is…well, irresistible.

"You asked me to your office to discuss *us?*"

"Was that not one of the options on your little list?"

"No," she says. "Never even crossed my mind."

"Well," I say, making my voice a dark drawl. "I can't very well have you attacking me again where your brother might catch us."

Her eyes flash. "Attack you!"

"First, the strip poker," I say. "And then the kiss in the kitchen. I'd say you were playing with fire, Blair, if I'd think it would have any effect on you."

Her gaze deepens at the mention of the game of strip poker. Though I keep my face impassive, it stirs me too.

The image of Blair on the couch dressed in nothing but her underwear and the fall of her hair comes back to me. With the firelight flicking across her golden skin, it's an image I'll carry with me until the end of my days.

"That's why you wanted to meet in your office? You think you're safe here?"

"Safe enough," I say, daring her to object.

A slow shake of her head as she comes to some understanding. I curse myself, watching her formulate her words. She's always seen more than I'd wanted her to. "You're hoping I'll back out of this," she says quietly. "But why?" She speaks again before I have to, her voice lighter. "Getting to know one another, then. I'll have to retract my claws until later."

The heat of her voice makes me want to shake my head at the

same time as need claws up my spine. Fuck, but I want this woman, against reason and common sense itself.

Her voice turns playful, the voice I've heard her use so many times with Cole and Skye and her coterie of friends. Never with me. "So, I have questions."

"Of course you do." It's a groan, really. But perhaps I could use this to my advantage. Make her see the man I am—make her walk away.

"How come Cole's never spoken about your family?"

"Next question," I say.

"But that's an easy one," she protests. "You can't dodge them all, you know, not if we're to get to know one another."

Not the getting-to-know *I had in mind,* I think, and maybe she sees it on my face, because her lip curls.

"So you want easier ones, huh? Fine." She leans forward. "What's your favorite color?"

My lips curve, too. "So we moved from the psychologist's couch to fourth-grade recess in the span of one conversation, did we?"

"Maybe if you weren't so hard to get to know, I wouldn't have to resort to such extreme measures."

"I don't have a favorite color."

"Good. I'm glad we established that. See, don't you already feel like we're much better friends?"

I roll my eyes. "You're absolutely ridiculous."

"And now you're learning things about me. This is great." She tries to hide her smile by biting her lower lip. If I'd found her beautiful before, she's glorious now. Alight from within. "Tell me why you started your firm."

It's the last thing I expect her to ask. I suspect a trap, but in her honey-brown eyes there's nothing but sincerity. I find myself answering more honestly than I'd planned.

"I wanted to make a name for myself. And I wanted to make money. Loads and loads of it."

There's no censure in her face at the blatant admittance of

greed. Instead, she nods thoughtfully. "You and Cole must have bonded over that, at university."

I snort. "Cole's a builder. He always wanted to leave a mark, a legacy. For me it wasn't quite like that."

"Why this specific industry, then?"

Why do you do something so distasteful? Is that her question? I square my shoulders and look past her. "I was good at it. I still am."

She nods, like I've given her something to think about. I don't like that. "Why fashion?" I ask her instead. There's no doubt in my mind that she could have picked anything, anything at all. With her smile and intellect, with her family's money and background, any avenue must have been open for her.

Her lips turn down in a frown at my question. Does she think I'm judging?

"It's what I've always enjoyed. It was what I dreamed of since I was a kid. And… I felt like I had to at least try, you know? I had to know before I decided to switch lanes."

It's not quite an answer to my question. There's more there, things that probably have to do with that line she launched a few years ago, but she moves the conversation on before I have a chance to press. "Look at us being so civil," she points out. "A few weeks ago, I wouldn't have believed it."

"Me neither."

"Why *did* you hate me for so long?" She gets up from her chair, coming around the desk to my side. "You never did tell me."

"You're asking what my version of your poker game was?" It's a question to buy time. There's no way I can tell her the truth, painful and unearned as it is. *I had to stay away from you, and the best way to do that was to make* you *want to stay away.*

"Yes."

"Perhaps that's just who I am," I murmur. "Perhaps it wasn't you—perhaps I'm just like that with everyone."

Her eyes widen slightly. Had she never considered that? My

reputation is most certainly earned. There's a reason people call me a vulture with relish.

"Not with my brother. Not with his wife."

"I've known Cole a long time."

She cocks her head. "Some would assume you'd be nice to your best friend's little sister, you know."

"Keeping you at arm's length *was* me being nice."

Her eyes dance. "I think we have different opinions of nice."

"Clearly."

"I have more questions."

"I don't doubt that you do."

Her teeth worry her lip, but the look in her eyes is entirely playful. It's overwhelming, facing the full brunt of her mischievous flirtation. She's always dazzled in social situations—no wonder she's invited to more parties and events than she can ever attend.

"What about André?" I force my voice to grow steely. "Have you lost interest in the boy?"

Her smile widens. "I broke up with him months ago."

I turn my gaze toward the windows. So she'd toyed with my expectations instead, without admitting that he was nothing to her. Drawing out my jealousy, even as I insulted her and pushed her away. Clever.

"Which leads me to another one of my questions. *Why* are the only women I've ever seen you spend time with the ones who only care for your money?" She steps closer, and the teasing in her voice gives way to earnestness. "It seems hollow."

"Like sipping champagne with fellow heiresses night after night?"

The barb hit home. Blair's eyes widen, and then narrow in anger. Her hatred of being portrayed as spoiled or indulgent is something I know well. An easy wound to press.

But she doesn't fight.

"Yes," she says instead. "Exactly as hollow as that."

"Perhaps I prefer it that way." I take a sip of my brandy to gather my wits. The women I'd been with had never wanted anything but my notoriety, my edge, my money. They'd enjoyed it when I was rough in bed, wanting the man they thought Nicholas Park was. No one asked questions like these. *What about your family?* Bah.

The point of this had been to make Blair back off. To see that this was a bad idea.

I hadn't succeeded at all.

Blair steps closer. A lock of her hair falls forward and she pushes it back impatiently. "I don't believe that for a second."

"Believe what you wish." I make my words deliberately cold, looking away from her as if she's not inches from my face. For years, my unfeeling facade had worked with her. All attempts of reaching out had been rebuffed like this. I wait in pained silence for her irritation, for her turning away.

"Damn it, Nick, you're making this far harder than it needs to be." Her eyes blaze with anger, her hands clasped into fists at her side. But as I watch, the anger flares and morphs into fierce determination.

And then she attacks me.

There is no other way to describe it. She forces her way into the circle of my arms, a living flame come to life, her lips warm against mine. There's no finesse to it. Perhaps that's why it overwhelms me so. My body had already been on the edge from her nearness, and with her warm scent crashing into me, my dams break.

I catch her around the waist. It's nothing at all to pull her against my body, her soft breasts giving way against my chest. The kisses she gives me are fierce with determination. The message is clear.

As if you like it hollow!

My hands gripping her waist, I take control of the kiss. *I'll give you more than you bargained for,* it says. Her mouth opens against my tongue and her body melts into mine as I push her against the desk.

Just like last time, and the time before that, kissing is a far better language for us. Words are unnecessary when her arms twine around my neck. This says everything and more.

And hollow it is not.

Not for all in the world can I imagine letting her go. How could I, when she's soft and warm and so willing and I'm drowning in this, in her, in the sensations—

"Mr. Park? You have a phone call."

"Damn it," I curse, reaching past her to press down on the answering intercom on my desk. "Take a message," I bark.

Blair giggles, her hands coming down to rest on my chest. "What awful timing he has," she says, reaching up to kiss my neck.

I push her back. "Not here."

She rocks back on her heels with a pout, but nods. "All right. Where, then?"

"So eager, Blair?"

She reaches out and runs a finger over the edge of my jaw. The simple touch sends a shiver through me, and she sees that. "I think we both are," she murmurs. "This has been a long time coming."

Eight years, to be exact.

"I'll figure something out," I say. "Now, will you be able to behave yourself in the future?"

"Behave myself?"

"No attacks," I say, raising an eyebrow. "Consider your brother's house neutral territory."

"It's Switzerland," she agrees warmly. Her eyes dance as she looks up at me. Finally, I think—I'm finally seeing the Blair that she shows to other people. The Blair who has so much lightness in her that it spills out at the seams. I doubt I'm worthy of the sight, but damn if it doesn't warm me regardless.

"Behave yourself," I murmur again, bending my head to press a final kiss to her full lips. She sighs into the kiss, warm, trusting, lovely. I straighten just as she steps closer.

"Not here," I say darkly. "You'd better leave, before I completely lose my head."

"And that would be a bad thing?"

"Oh, it definitely would."

She heads to the door, pausing before it. Her lips are curved. "So we'll get to know one another… better."

And damn it, but how can I not give her what she wants when it's what I'm dying for as well? "Yes," I agree. "We will."

13

BLAIR

"But that's the thing," Maddie says triumphantly. "It *didn't* work! So now they're stuck renovating the entire property regardless, and it's not usable until spring."

The rest of us laugh obediently, John shooting Maddie a particularly warm smile.

"So your family is out of a chalet this winter," Tate says. "How tragic."

"You should organize a fundraiser," I suggest dryly. "It's a charitable cause."

That gets genuine laughter. Maddie elbows me playfully. "Only if you promise to be the hostess."

As the conversation continues, my eyes sweep the fashionable crowd. The Seattle Fashion Institute has decided to celebrate the opening of New York Fashion Week remotely. A highlight reel is running on a giant projector screen, and below the giant catwalks, Seattle's fashion-interested sip on champagne.

It's a room that younger me would have loved being in. But ever since the fashion disaster that was my first line, I'm uncomfortably aware of what some of the experts in the room probably think of me.

Sipping my champagne, I glance around the room and the illustrious attendees.

That's when I see him. Nick, casually leaning against the opposite wall, a glass of brandy in hand. In the dim lighting, his suit looks like poured ink on his large frame. His eyes sweep the crowd like a predator's before they lock with mine.

What's he doing here?

I raise my champagne glass in greeting.

He inclines his head, his lips half-curled. There's something in his gaze, something I want to explore further, but then he looks down at a woman approaching him. Long dark hair, an asymmetric dress. I force myself to look away.

The conversation continues around me but it's just words now, words I have difficulty following. When I glance back to Nick, he's gone, and so is the woman he was talking to. The champagne burns pleasurably down my throat.

"Excuse me for a moment." I weave through the crowd with practiced ease. Several people stop me to talk, and I do my best to be in the moment, but my eyes can't seem to stop roving. Why the hell is he here?

Was this what he meant by *figuring something out?*

I curse my heels as I walk up the steps to the calmer mezzanine. No Amazon-sized models walking here, and no house music either. Is he here?

An arm wraps around my waist and then I'm pulled unceremoniously into a coat closet. The scent of him is what hits me first, what keeps me from shrieking.

"Nick?"

He shuts the door firmly behind us. "That's the one."

"Why are you here?"

"Are you complaining?"

"No." With his arm still around me, I'm pressed tightly against his body. My hands slide up his chest of their own accord.

"Good." He bends his head and presses his lips to mine. It's just as heady and intoxicating as I've gotten used to. How can every kiss with him feel like the first?

His tongue demands entry and the deepening of the kiss

opens something in my chest, something I'd already been on the verge of feeling. Affection, more of it than my stupid crush on him had ever commanded before.

"What's this?" I tease. "What happened to Mr. I-like-it-hollow?"

"Consider this a tactical retreat," he says, tipping my head back to run his lips along my jaw. "I have to attack first or you'd be out there, wrapped around me for all to see."

"Oh? You're that irresistible, are you?"

"To you, I seem to be," he mutters. And then he's kissing me again and all I can do is hold on and ride the sensations. Kissing him back, nipping at his lower lip, tugging at his hair and hearing him groan into my mouth.

"Why are you here tonight?"

"Isn't that obvious?" His hands skate down the sides of my body, smoothing over the silk of my dress. "I can't have you throw yourself at me in the office. I certainly can't have you throw yourself at me in your brother's house."

"Throw myself at you?" I try to make my voice dry, but it comes out as a purr.

"You know exactly what you've been doing." He kisses down my neck. There's tension in his shoulders, in his chest, strong and coiled beneath my hands. I wonder what he'd be like unleashed—when all that energy has a focus and a purpose. The thought makes me shiver.

"What is it you want from me, Blair?" he demands. His hands tug gently on my hair and my eyes flit up to meet his. "You've been teasing me for weeks. Do you just want to see how far I can be pushed? You know I'll push back. I told you that I'm not a man who plays games. So if this is a game, Blair, I'll end it."

The kiss he gives me then is a blazing, furious thing. I kiss him back and hold on as he turns us around, until my back is against the rack of coats. He disappears for a moment and I hear the *click* of a lock being turned. The sound sends shivers of nervous anticipation through me.

"Can't be your first time sneaking away at an event." It's meant to be empty bluster, but it comes out as a question.

"You're making assumptions," he says.

"It's the only thing I can do," I respond. "I know so little about you."

He reaches out and tips my head back. My breath quickens at the intensity in his eyes. "You know plenty."

"Not enough."

"More than enough," he says. "And you still want this?"

I wet my lips. "What's *this?*"

"Don't play dumb."

I step closer, my body reacting to the heat emanating off of him. "To finish what we started during the strip poker game, you mean. To get to know one another."

His eyes move from my eyes to my lips. "Yes."

There's something in the tone of his voice—he wants my agreement, my acceptance, my permission. I give it to him.

"I always finish what I start."

His eyes flash and then he's kissing me, bending his head to meet my lips. Slow, languorous, teasing kisses, his mouth a hard press against mine. Kisses that say he'll take his time—that he's done this before, that he's in control. I don't want Nick to be in control.

I want him to lose it.

I kiss him with my arms wrapped around his neck and my breasts pressed to his chest. I melt into him, opening my mouth for his tongue, fingers tugging at the hair on the nape of his neck. Shivers are coursing through my body like electricity.

Strong hands grip my waist. He's kissing me with expert skill, and I'm doing the same.

Surrender, his kisses say.

Give up, mine say.

My hands find the buttons of his shirt. It doesn't take long to undo them all, finding the strength and width of his chest beneath. The dark smattering of hair. I let my hands run underneath his shirt, hanging off him.

His hand strokes from my hip to my breast, palming it. My nipple is hard through the thin fabric and his thumb brushes over it once, twice, sending heady want through me. Even through my clothes, the touch is like fire. I want him to twist it, to soothe the ache.

Nick understands. He tugs my blouse up with strong movements and tosses it to the side without looking.

"I recognize this," he says darkly, hands on my bare waist, eyes on my bra. It's one of my own—the one I'd worn to the strip poker game in Whistler.

I arch my back invitingly and he understands, large hands tugging the cups of my bra down to bare my nipples. His mouth is there an instant later and warm heat spreads from the contact, rippling through me. I run my hands over his hair and bite my lip to keep from moaning.

Nick's voice is gravelly. "Do you know how hard it was to keep from doing this during the poker game?"

I nod, realizing too late that he can't see me. "So hard."

He gives a low chuckle. "That it was."

I reach back and undo my bra. The only thing I want is skin against skin, to feel the heat of him against me.

"Tell me you're also wearing the same panties as that night. The image of you in them has haunted me." His hand ventures down to my skirt.

"Why don't you check?"

And God help me, but he does. His right hand lifts the hem of my skirt with ease and then he's there, touching my upper thighs and easing my legs apart.

"Fuck, Blair…"

I *am* wearing a similar pair of underwear. Beige with lacy flowers in the lining, the fabric almost transparent. His fingers slip under the lace, roughness of his fingertips against my sensitive skin.

I hold my breath as his fingers move further down and then he's *there*, touching me, and my entire body shivers at the intimate touch.

The pressure and the *oh-so-amazing* circling of his fingers are too much for me to watch. I close my eyes and lean my head against his shoulder, losing myself to the sensations. His voice is a hoarse growl in my ear.

"Do you know how much I wanted to do this during that fucking poker game? A thin piece of fabric was the only thing separating me from this."

And then he's delving deeper, parting and stroking and one long finger sinks into me with ease. The simple movement steals my breath away.

Lips on my neck, fingers inside me, his left hand on my breast. I'm caught between currents and do my best to hold on, but Nick won't let me. Why was I fighting against his skill earlier, against his experience? It seems futile now.

Nick in control is a glorious thing.

He turns me around, his left arm locking around my bare waist like a steel band. I'm held against his body, no way out, no mercy.

"That's it," he murmurs against my skin, his fingers speeding up, circling faster.

Perhaps a stronger woman than me could resist, but I can't, not with so many sensations at once. He presses his lips to that spot right where my neck meets my shoulder and I breathe in the scent of him, of man and leather and musk and I'm hovering right on the edge.

"Let go," he orders me, and my traitorous body does. His hand slaps down between my legs and the sting against my arousal sends me over the edge. I tumble and fall into pleasure. It's so effortless that even in the midst of my orgasm a small part of my mind recognizes this for the unusual thing it is.

He holds me as I shatter and piece myself back together, big hands still moving over my body, on my breasts, my waist, my thighs. That's when I feel him against me—a hardness against my back. I roll my hips against it and Nick groans in response.

Can we, here? Now?

If my body was the one calling the shots, he'd already be

buried inside me. I'm aching for him. I twist in his arms and he lets me, finding his lips with my own.

Our movements quicken. His shirt is easily pushed off and then his body is finally mine to touch. The warm skin, the rippling of strong muscles under skin, the impossibly wide shoulders.

All mine.

And maybe I tell him that because he smiles, the same sardonic grin as always, and tugs at my skirt. "This damn thing won't come off," he groans. "I'll be yours as soon as it's off."

I undo the hidden zipper at the same time as I nod to his pants. "And those."

Watching one another, we strip off until we're in nothing but our underwear. I reach out, wanting to uncover him, to see the bulge unclothed, but his hands stop me again. They smooth over my hips and grab hold of the thin fabric of my underwear.

"There's no going back from this, Blair."

I roll my eyes at him. "How many times are you going to warn me tonight, Nick? Are you getting cold feet?"

He snorts. "Nothing about me is cold right now."

I shake out my hair and smile at the way his eyes catch the movement. Shimmying my hips in his grasp, I make my decision. "Take them off."

He pulls my panties down my legs and it's like a lever has been pulled, or a dam broken, because there is not the least bit of hesitation left in him. His movements are businesslike, strong, gripping.

"Brace your hands against the wall."

I do what he says and for a moment the backs of my thighs are cold until he's there, thighs against mine, hands smoothing over my bare skin.

"Fuck," he says, and the curse strengthens me. I arch my back and push against him, hearing him swear again. He gives my cheek a light slap and then he's running something along my skin, something hot and hard and I want to turn around to see but he's gripping me tightly.

There's power in this—in giving myself to *his* power. Surrendering to the attraction between us. How long had I wanted to see him like this? Unchained and unfettered, the real Nick below the cool facade.

Anticipation and fear chase one another through my body, reacting to his teasing, to the slow stroke of him, waiting for the delicious sensation of his entry.

And then he's there. He pushes into me slowly, an inch at a time, his hands on my hips. He's big, bigger than I'm used to, and I breathe through the overwhelming sensations.

He pauses. "You okay?"

"Yes, yes, yes…" I take a deep breath and relax into the feeling. I reach back, a hand on his hip, wanting to pull him all the way in. He gives it to me, burying himself to the hilt with a groan.

His hands brace on either side of me as he stills. "Fucking hell," he mutters.

I feel the same. The fit is too snug, it's too much, but I think I'd die if he pulled out and left me.

He doesn't. He starts to move instead and I do my best to hold on, closing my eyes at the delicious invasion. The thrusts are teasing. Slow, deep, controlled. One of his hands slip from its grip on my hip to settle between my legs. His fingers circle in tune to his movements.

I fist my hand blindly in one of the coats on the rack and bite my lip again to keep from crying out.

"God," he groans. "You're so tight."

It's undeniably true, at least compared to the sheer size of him. I push my hips back to meet his thrusts. The sweet, now-fading pain makes my pleasure build faster, reignited by his hands.

So when I turn my head back to see him, his eyes wild and burning, his hands gripping my hips, the words fall easily from my lips. "Don't hold back."

And let it never be said that Nick didn't obey, not this time. His thrusts speed up. His hands grip until my skin stings, and still, I want him to grip me harder. My hands claw for support against the wall.

His body covers mine completely. The heavy, deep breathing from him echoes my own, driving on my pleasure. This is what I want from him—to see him come apart, to see him undone, for him to lose himself in me.

Just like I've been lost in him so many times.

He gives me that. He pumps fast and strong, and I feel powerful *and* used, and somehow the two strengthen one another rather than detract. His need is palpable and I'm the only thing that can give him relief, our bodies fitting together perfectly.

It doesn't take long for either of us. The years of irritation and wanting and banter have become a living thing, a fuel to our fire, layering this encounter with more meaning than I'd expected.

Nick pulls me up against his body as his hips work erratically into me. The feeling of him pulsing inside pushes me over the edge. It's a blaze of glory and sweat and connection, our bodies plastered together, my back to his front.

My heart is still pounding as we come apart. His arms are around me, turning me around, pulling me into an embrace.

"You okay?"

I nod against the warmth of his shoulder. "Are you?"

A low, dark laugh. "I doubt I've ever been *more* okay."

Something giddy and inappropriate dances in my chest. It feels like elation… or perhaps happiness. "I can't believe we just did that."

"You can't? I can't believe we waited so long." Nick runs a hand over my hair in a gesture that's more sweet than sensual. This is a side of him I've never seen. More disarmed, and less… wary.

"So is this why you came to a Fashion Week event?" I say. "Were you even invited?"

"I'm invited everywhere," he scoffs. "All it takes is a few phone calls."

"Mhm."

"Besides, I couldn't let you spend all your time with those sycophants out there."

"My *friends*, who will probably be wondering where I am." I rise on my tiptoes and press a soft, sweet kiss to his lips. He lets me. "Let's go. We're… oh God. I can't believe we actually did this in a coat closet."

"You leave first." He reaches for his clothes. Despite his nakedness and the small room, he looks the picture of control and ease. "I'll leave in a bit."

"So concerned with our reputations," I say.

"Only with yours," he says. "Now, will this stop you from throwing yourself at me?"

I fasten my bra and glare at him through my sideswept bangs. His cool tone is quickly bringing out my temper. "I was never *throwing* myself at you."

"Call it whatever you will. But I'm expecting perfect behavior tomorrow at your brother's."

"You're coming to dinner, too?"

"Yes." He looks at me like he's daring me to protest. Does he think I still dislike him? Perhaps he does. He's basically insinuating he just threw me a bone, yes, *that bone,* to stop me from jumping him.

"Come on, quit acting like this wasn't for your own benefit, too." I tug my skirt into place and arch a brow at him. "Your pleasure was pretty damn evident."

His eyes narrow. "So was yours. By my count, you came twice, Blair."

Of course Nicholas Park is the sort of man to gloat about that. If only he knew how rare that was for me.

"It was adequate," I say breezily.

"Adequate?" He motions for me to turn around as he tucks my shirt in. "You wound me."

"Hardly."

"I'll just have to aim for three next time."

"Next time?" I step away from his large hands and shake out my hair, knowing how he likes that. The smile I throw his way is

113

the same one I've always given him when we spar. "So you're that sure there'll be one?"

Nick narrows his eyes at me, but I don't give him a chance to respond. I unlock the door and slip out of the closet instead, the scent of him still clinging to my skin, my heart beating a wild dance in my ribcage.

14

BLAIR

My brother's house used to be a safe place. Dinner there was easy, fun, comfortable. It was family and food and laughter. Tonight is nothing like that. It's nerves and expectation and this strange, giddy excitement, knowing that Nick will be there.

I take my time preparing for dinner. Putting on old-school music and trying on dresses, wanting to strike a perfect balance between cute and sexy. I'd promised Nick I'd behave myself, and I would. But that didn't mean I wouldn't try to tempt him. There was no rule about *him* not attacking *me*, was there?

I'm whistling to myself as I do my makeup. I've done two months out of three for my consulting contract for his firm. B.C. Adams is doing better than it has in a decade, though it's too early to tell if it's out of the woods yet. My brother is having a baby. I've finally—*finally*—slept with Nicholas Park after a near decade of wondering what it would be like.

It had been hard. It had been fast.

And it had been every bit as exciting as I'd always imagined. In a coat closet, nonetheless. That was definitely a first, and even if a small part of me is outraged at my own daring, the rest is… well, pretty damn impressed.

Skye is the first to grab a hold of me when I arrive. From the living room, I hear my brother and Nick talking, but she drags me in the opposite direction.

"Oh my god, Blair, they're *amazing.*"

It takes me a moment to understand. "What's amazing? Oh, you mean the samples?"

"Yes! I'm wearing your underwear now and one of your slips." She looks down at the navy dress she's wearing, and then laughs at herself. "Well, it's not like you can see that. But I've been using the negligees too. Everything you gave me."

Gratitude makes my chest warm. "Thank you, Skye. Truly."

"How've you made lace this comfortable?"

"It's actually the mixture of material. Elastane and polyamide and cotton, all in the right percentages."

"Well, don't change it," she says firmly. "I'm writing down a list of notes too, with all my thoughts. I'll give you extensive feedback."

"That's exactly what I want. Thank you."

"How long is this a secret?" She glances toward the cased opening and the voices that beckon. "Cole has wondered, you know, about my sudden influx of new underwear. And not negatively, either."

I close my eyes. "Ugh. I didn't want to hear that."

She laughs. "Come on, you already know I'm pregnant. How do you think that happened, huh?"

"Why are you continuing this line of conversation?"

"Sorry, sorry. You look a bit green. Do you need to sit down? Should I fetch my smelling salts?"

I roll my eyes at her version of exaggeration. "You read too many Regency novels. *Smelling salts,* Christ."

"Clearly something we should bring back." Her arm twines under mine. Shorter than me and with her brown hair, we look like nothing alike, and yet she feels like a true sister.

"So," she says, her eyes sweeping over my dress. "Are you going out later?"

"I don't think so, no."

"Well, you look like a million bucks," she says. I glance

down, and oh my poor heart is vain, but I feel strengthened by her compliment. A short gray dress contrasted with a knitted sweater. Stockings and boots and my hair soft around my shoulders. It's a fall look, designed to show off my legs.

"Thank you," I say, winking. "I dressed up for you."

Skye rolls her eyes. "Liar. But if that makes you feel more comfortable, I won't press you for the true reason."

My words falter in my mouth. I want to ask her to explain herself—does she know about Nick and me?—but we're walking into the living room and the chance is lost.

There's no way she suspects. What Skye knows, she'd tell Cole, and my brother is still beautifully oblivious. He wouldn't be able to hide it.

He sweeps me into a hug, tweaking my nose when he leans back—he knows I hate that under the *best* of circumstances. And with Nicholas Park, who not twenty-four hours ago was inside of me, observing the exchange is *not* the best of circumstances.

Cole's smile is wide. "Apparently you're *excellent* at what you do at Nick's firm."

My eyes flit past his shoulder to lock on Nick's. He doesn't look away. "I am?"

"Yes," Cole continues. "I pretended to be surprised, but of course I wasn't."

"Of course," I repeat dazedly. Nick nods his hello to me before taking another sip of his drink. His face is impassive again, no hint of amusement in his eyes and no sardonic smile lurking in the corner of his mouth.

"Not to mention that you're both here together and we didn't have to trick you or hold you here under duress." Cole's smile is still wide.

No, he definitely doesn't suspect anything.

"Progress," Nick intones, raising his glass as a toast to me. I feel burned by the intensity in his gaze. *Play along,* it says. *You promised to behave.*

"Progress," I echo.

The sound of footsteps on the staircase breaks us out of our staring contest. Timmy comes barreling down, Skye's nephew, a boy of fourteen. Puberty has just started to grab a hold of the boy and his gangly limbs are longer every time I see him.

He stops next to his aunt. "I heard dinner was done."

"So it is." She reaches up and pushes his hair back. They're almost the same height now. "I booked a time at the hairdresser tomorrow. Your hair is really getting too long."

A faint blush spreads across Timmy's cheeks. He pushes her hand away. "Hi, Blair," he says to me.

I smile at him. He often spends the night at Skye and Cole's place, and they've given him his own room. "Hey, kid. How's it going?"

"Good." He comes up beside me. "Cole and I just managed to get tickets for the World Series." His voice cracked once, faintly.

"What, really?"

"Yes." His wide grin is infectious. The discussion takes up a fair amount of bandwidth around the dinner table, with both Nick and Cole chiming in. Skye sends me a commiserating look across the table. Neither she nor I have ever been able to cultivate any true interest in baseball.

Nick and Cole smile, too, at the occasional crack in Timmy's voice. It's only after dinner, when he scampers back upstairs to his new video game—my brother spoils him beyond belief—that they both laugh.

"I remember that," Nick says. "Thank God it only lasts a few months, at best."

"Cole's voice cracked for at least a year." I sink deeper into the armchair, nodding to where my brother is sitting with his arm around Skye.

"Really?" she asks.

"Oh, yes. And Lairy didn't let me live that down, either."

Nick sits in the armchair beside mine. His dark eyes find mine. "Can you really be that cruel?"

I cross my legs and feel a slice of triumph as his eyes take in the movement. The dress had been an excellent choice. "Sometimes."

"She was merciless," Cole adds. "But I've teased her about a fair number of things too, so I'd say we're even."

"Even?" I feign mock outrage. "Any younger sibling knows that there's no such thing as even. Skye, help me out."

She nods sagely. "They can tickle you, you can't tickle them. They can tease you, you can't tease them. I'm with Blair here. You had to take every chance you got."

"Show no mercy, take no hostages," I say. And then, because I can't resist, I turn to Nick. "Do you have any siblings? Help us convince Cole."

The shake of his head is smooth. "Only child, I'm afraid."

"What a wonderful thing," Cole sighs, and we all laugh as I pretend to flip him off.

"To be fair, you gave me a lot of things *to* tease you about. You made it easy, Lairy."

"Are you victim-blaming?" I shake my head at my big brother in mock outrage. "I'd advise you to stop talking right about now."

"Or what? You're going to get our lawyers involved? We have the same ones." He laughs good-naturedly and reaches out to rest his arm around Skye's shoulder. "You had a crush on a new guy every week. It was great fodder for jokes."

Skye and Nick both laugh. I don't, the smile on my face growing just a tad tighter. "You kept bringing your friends over. It was very easy to." My voice is carefully cheerful. My mingling voice, honed by years of parties. Inside, I'm trying to telepathically tell my brother to *shut the hell up.*

Skye takes a sip of her alcohol-free cider. "As if you didn't have crushes when you were a teenager."

Cole leans his head back against the couch. He looks the picture of ease, at peace and amused. Shouldn't people who've found their happiness be kind? Not, you know, *ruin it for others?* My brother hasn't gotten that memo, because he destroys everything.

"Not like Blair did. Didn't you have a crush on Nick when we first became friends?"

Several things happen at once, then.

In my peripheral view, I see Nick still.

Skye frowns at her husband in clear disapproval.

Cole grins at me and Nick, thinking this is nothing but a fun joke. Something we'll laugh about.

I force my voice to obey. It comes out unhurried, unforced. "That was such a long time ago," I say. "And it lasted for exactly a week."

"Until you discovered what a brute he is." Cole nods to Nick, his smile growing wider.

Nick smiles back. It's his sardonic one, the one that says he's laughing at his own private joke. "Not fit for anyone's little sister," he says.

"Exactly." Cole takes a sip of his own whiskey and glances down at Skye. Her displeasure is still plain, and as he sees it, he pauses. "What?"

She shakes her head at him, but thankfully doesn't say anything.

"Should we turn the tables?" I ask instead. "Who was the one who crashed Dad's old Corvette a month after he got his license?"

Cole groans and Nick latches on to the story immediately, asking for details. I breathe a shaky sigh of relief, even though I know it's only temporary.

There's no way Nick will let me live this down.

And somehow, when it's time to leave, Nick is the one who stands and faces me. "I'll drive you home," he says.

The walk to his car is silent. I glance at him twice from the corner of my eye, but he looks like he's retreated, back into the cold impassivity I'd been used to for years.

I repress a sigh as I climb into the passenger seat of his Land Rover. "Come on. Didn't we behave ourselves perfectly in there? I kept my promise."

He nods.

"And?" I let the word drawl. "Don't we both get a gold star?"

His hands grip the wheel tightly as he pulls out of my brother's driveway. We pause on the other side of the gate, blocking the way while the giant wrought-iron gates close behind us. Always security-minded.

"So you had a crush on me." His voice is tight. "What an interesting little tidbit."

"You can't just ignore that, can you? Pretend you never heard it?"

"Not likely, Blair."

"It was a long time ago," I say. There's no need for him to know all the gory details—that the crush had lingered throughout the years, that every time I'd seen him it had reawakened and kept me wishing.

"So it had nothing to do with yesterday? With the last couple weeks of..." His voice dies out, but I hear the words. *Of throwing yourself at me.*

Can you sink through a car with embarrassment? I'm about to, burning a hole through the steel until his expensive car becomes a Fred Flintstone vehicle.

A hundred different responses flit through my mind. Do I play it off as a joke, too? There's no way Nick will handle it well if I say *yes*.

"It had nothing to do with that," I say firmly. "I was what, eighteen when we met? No, it's in the past. Cole was an ass to bring it up, but it means nothing."

Nick releases a breath. "That's what I figured."

"Good," I say. "So I don't want you to worry. I'm not expecting anything to come from this." I cross my legs in the car, and his eyes dart to them again. *Victory,* I think, even as my heart beats with the word *defeat.*

He shifts lanes smoothly, passing by a slower car. "You have no expectations," he repeats.

"No."

"All right," he says, and somehow, it sounds like he's the injured party. "But I'll be damned if the one time I had you was at a party where I couldn't even hear you moan properly. So when we get to yours, I'm coming upstairs, and I'm going to make you count how many times you come tonight. I'm aiming for a minimum of three."

My breath whooshes out of my chest at that. There are no words in response to that declaration, none at all. I can't even form thoughts.

He reaches out and puts a hand on my thigh. I look at it there, at the broad, tan skin and the curl of his fingers. "Are *you* attacking *me*, Mr. Park?"

The curl of his lips is back. "You'll recognize it when I do," he says. And when we park outside my apartment building… well, he follows me up.

15

BLAIR

Nick follows me into my apartment with a hand on my low back. Nerves and excitement dance through me.

I feel alive—I feel powerful.

His eyes scan the apartment in quiet perusal. For so many years it's been completely unthinkable that he would ever be here. An alien visit to Earth felt far likelier than Nick Park and me alone together in my home.

And yet, here we are.

The building is one of Cole's early projects, and like so many things in my life, it's not something I worked to gain myself. Is he judging me for that?

"This is a nice place."

Nick walks to the giant windows in my living room. They overlook the city, and not for the first time, I wish I could read his mind.

"Do you want a glass of brandy?"

"If you have it, yes. Sure."

I search through my makeshift bar cart in the corner, fishing out a bottle that Cole must have left here sometime. It'll have to do. I walk past my study on the way back to him—it's simple enough to close the door with my foot. There's no reason he should see the mess of clothing samples in there.

Nick turns to me. His eyes sweep over my form again, and this time, there's no hiding the want in them.

"Here," I say softly, handing him the drink.

"Your place looks exactly like I expected it to."

"And what was that?"

He swirls the amber-colored liquid around in his glass as he speaks. "Organized chaos."

I glance around, seeing the space as he might. The oriental carpet, the beige sofa, the colorful chandelier. It's an eclectic mix of everything I like.

"That's me," I say. "Organized but chaotic."

"So I'm learning."

"What's your place like?" I take a step back, sweeping my gaze over his six-foot-two form just as appraisingly as he just had. Dressed in all black, with his dark hair and even darker eyes… "Let me guess. It's utilitarian. Nothing frivolous, nothing unnecessary."

His lip curls. "Are you making assumptions again, Blair?"

"I have to. I told you, I know so little about you."

He reaches out and tips my head back. My breath quickens at the intensity in his eyes. "And I told you—you know plenty."

A million questions flit through my mind. Why does he keep everyone at an arm's—no, a *football-field's*—length distance? There's so much I want to know, and nothing I can ask.

I step closer, reaching up to run my hand tentatively through his short, dark hair. It's silky to the touch. "It wasn't hollow at all," I murmur, running my nails over his scalp. "Us, I mean. In the closet."

The furrow in his brow relaxes. How easy it would be, I think, if our communication was only done by touch.

"No, it wasn't." His hands close around my hips, dipping his head. "And it won't be this time either."

He kisses me forcefully, expertly, punctuating his words. Desire sweeps through me with the touch of his lips, the brief intrusion of his tongue, the power coiled in his muscles.

He's more man than anyone I've been with before.

I take his glass and break apart just long enough to set both of ours down. He keeps his gaze locked on mine the entire time. Can dark eyes swim with need? His seem to.

Nick's hands skim down my sides and grips my thighs, lifting me up. "Bedroom?"

"Down the hall."

The ease with which he carries me completely sweeps away my resolution to make *him* come undone—my great plan for turning the tables this time. To wrest control away from him.

Because why would I want to stop him from doing his thing when it's *this* good?

He climbs onto the bed and lays me down, all without letting go of me. My head lands between two cushions and I reach up to toss them off the bed impatiently.

"Christ. How many decorative pillows do you need?"

"It's not important." I twist beneath him so I can wrap my legs around his waist, rolling my hips once, twice…

He's still glaring above my head like my pillows are a personal affront. "It's like a shrine to comfort. Ridiculous."

I put my finger on his chin and tilt his head back down to mine. "I distinctly remember being promised three orgasms."

"Are you telling me to keep my head in the game?" The faint injury in his voice is too much for me. I burst into laughter.

Nick rises up on his arms and looks down at me. A smile tugs at his lips. "Well, that wasn't supposed to happen."

Still grinning, I reach up to cup his face in my hands. "Sorry, sorry."

"A woman laughing in bed." He shakes his head in mock affront and bends to kiss my neck.

"The horror," I mumble. His lips trace my collarbone and it's increasingly hard to think.

"I need to step up my game." His hand bunches up the hem of my dress. Kissing his way down my body, he starts raising it inch by inch, my exposed skin his for the taking. I look up at the ceiling when he settles in between my legs.

Soft kisses to my inner thighs, warm, large hands smoothing

up my skin. He tugs my panties to the side and then he's there, mouth on me, and I close my eyes at the feeling. Relax, I tell myself. Just relax.

He stops. "What's wrong?"

"Nothing." I reach down to run my fingers over his hair. "Nothing at all."

"Every muscle in your body just locked up."

I force out a breath. "I'm not… good at enjoying that particular act."

Nick frowns. Framed by my bare thighs and still in his button-down shirt, the view is overwhelming. "Why not?"

God, this is *mortifying*. Other guys never noticed that I didn't particularly enjoy it. Why did he have to be different?

"I just… I can't get out of my head." Grabbing one of the offensive pillows, I clasp it over my head. "I never have. I'm just thinking about how you must be… well, waiting for me to finish, and that you might not enjoy it."

It's so embarrassing said out loud. The wish to take it back, to continue playing a strong and empowered and badass woman, is so overwhelming it nearly chokes me.

This certainly wasn't the easy sex he no doubt wanted.

The pillow is ripped away and then he's there, dark eyes burning. Is that anger? "Has a man ever told you that? Made you feel like that?"

Well, this just keeps getting worse, doesn't it? "Not in so many words," I say, "but… kind of?"

My first boyfriend never went down on me, and most other men had only done it in a perfunctory fashion. Like an appetizer they reluctantly had to get through before the main course.

"Fools," Nick says darkly.

"Yeah. Well, that's why, I guess."

Still watching me, Nick's hand starts stroking, right where his mouth had just been. Long fingers part and then circle. "But you enjoy this?"

I nod. Speaking is difficult when he's touching me—*oh*—right there.

Speculation dances in his gaze, and something else, something I recognize as the love of a challenge. He's always been one for impossible odds.

"Nick…" I warn, but it's no use. He settles back between my legs, but he doesn't use his mouth. He touches me leisurely instead.

"Do you know how much touching you turns me on?" His voice, usually gravelly, is a dark purr now. I reach for the pillow again and clutch it to my face.

His voice reaches me still, even as his fingers continue their sweet, sweet torture. "I'd imagined it, before the Fashion Week party. What it would feel like to do this."

And then his fingers dip lower and one sinks deliciously deep inside me. I push the pillow away, needing to see him, and the sight nearly breaks me.

His gaze is fixed between my legs and on the hand currently pleasuring me. "Fuck, Blair, you're so gorgeous."

The compliment rings in my head, the word bouncing in my skull. *Gorgeous*. My legs relax at the same time as my breathing grows faster.

"I won't go down on you again until you tell me I can," he continues, the heat of his breath washing over my skin. "But believe me when I tell you I want to. Your taste, the feel of you against my tongue…"

One of his hands reaches up to find my breast. My nipple is hard underneath the fabric of my bra and he pushes it away. Combined with his words, with the fingers he's using in me, on me…

"Yes," he murmurs. "That's it, Blair. You're so pretty here, you won't believe it, if only you knew…"

I don't think he knows what he's saying anymore, but it's okay, because I'm almost beyond hearing. Pleasure rises and crests and I shatter against his hand, my orgasm racing through me.

And all the while Nick continues touching me and watching me and murmuring something in a low voice. I force my breathing to slow enough to hear the words.

"Self-conscious," he's muttering. "A woman like this. Ridiculous."

As soon as my limbs work again, I reach for him. "Come here."

He climbs up my body with a faint shake of his head. "We're going to work on that," he vows, kissing me with a passion that reminds me that he hasn't gotten his release yet. And I kiss him back with everything I am.

We're going to work on this? That means he's predicting *more* of this, despite what he'd said in the car earlier.

I tug at his shirt. "Isn't it my time to make you fall apart?"

His smile is wicked. "I have no problem with receiving oral sex," he drawls. "I'd be happy to demonstrate."

I roll my eyes even as the impressive length of him presses against my stomach. His suggestion is interesting… Last time, I hadn't had a chance to even *see* it.

"Asking for pleasure." I shake my head in pretend censure, even as I push his shirt off. "Such bad manners."

"Not all of us were raised right."

I flip him around and he lets me, pulling me into a straddling position. "Say the magic word."

He tugs my bra off. "Now."

"No, that's not the one."

He falls back on the bed with a long-suffering sigh. "This is not a proportional response, Blair."

"It's that hard to say, is it?"

"No, it's just very, very hard." He rolls his hips for added emphasis, and yes, it most definitely is.

I decide to take pity on him. For one, I want to be in control. It's time to prove that this an equal playing field.

But more importantly… the smile on his face is one to keep.

"We'll have to work on your manners," I say, moving down to undo his zipper. He groans as my nails rake him through the fabric.

"*Please*," he says.

16

NICK

"*Please,*" I say. The word burns on the way out, but it's nothing compared to the now painful ache of my cock. Having tasted her, teased her, seen her…

I need her.

Blair smiles and pulls down the zipper to my pants. My view is even better from this angle—the curves of her collarbones, the glory of her round breasts, the flared hips. She's wearing nothing but those pathetically small panties, and they're still pushed to the side.

The perfection of her is near overwhelming. Seattle's golden socialite, perfect hostess, style icon.

She has a smattering of tiny birthmarks on her right hip. I know that now. I wonder how many others do.

Looking up at me, she runs her finger along the outline of my cock through my boxers. It feels good, but the smile on her face at my answering groan feels even better.

It chases away any lingering thoughts that I'd been too rough in the closet the other day. No, every time I'm foolish enough to think of Blair Porter as someone fragile, someone to be careful around, she disavows me of that notion.

She always goes toe to toe and eye to eye.

Blair finally pulls my boxers down and closes her hand

around me. The grip is teasing in its faintness, and I must have made some sort of sound, because she looks up at me.

"You're big," she comments. And damn it, but the matter-of-factness in her voice makes me feel ten feet tall. She's stating it like a fact—not a compliment.

"Yeah." The next words come through gritted teeth as she begins to stroke. "Did I hurt you the other day?"

"No," she says, and I resist the urge to smile. Blair would never admit to that, even if I had. "It'll just take getting used to."

Again, the swell of pure masculine pride that courses through me is overwhelming. It's not an emotion I'm proud of, but it's there, and damn if it doesn't make me grow even harder. "Something else we'll have to practice on," I say.

And then her hand is replaced by something warm and wet and I look down to find her lips around me.

It takes everything I am to force myself to lie still and endure. Golden hair spills around her, on my thighs and stomach, covering me in beauty. I reach out and it slips through my fingers like silk.

"Blair..."

She doesn't respond, but honey-brown eyes lift to meet mine. Seeing her like that is enough to send need pounding down my spine again. It's been a long time since I've wanted a woman this much.

"Fuck." The word slips out. She's moving faster now, and her mouth is enthusiastic and warm and damn when her tongue moves like that...

"See?" I mumble. "This is how you enjoy oral."

She releases me just long enough to shoot me a disparaging look. "Thank you, sensei," she says, her voice dripping with syrupy sarcasm, and I bark a laugh. Then her mouth is back and I'm not thinking anymore.

The urge to keep going is strong. To fist a hand in her hair, to take what she's offering for as long as it takes. The idea of finishing inside her mouth is enough to make my balls twitch.

But we have practicing to do. And it's Blair, and it's only the second time, and I'm supposed to show her why this is a good idea and should *absolutely* continue.

I reach down and grip her shoulders. I need her beneath me, her legs wrapped around me, to see her eyes as I push in.

"Inside you," I tell her. It's no effort at all to pull her up, her lithe body against mine. I tug her flimsy panties down her legs and off. Pretty as they are, she's far, far prettier.

But when I move to turn us over, she twists in my arms. "No."

She returns to her straddle instead. Seeing the protest in my eyes, she puts a hand on my chest and pushes. "*Stay.*"

I groan at the command but... amazingly, I obey. The angle does give me the most stunning visual as she rises up, gripping my cock, guiding it inside. I grab her hips and help her sink slowly down.

Inch after inch of me disappears.

I don't know what's best—the look in her eyes as I stretch her out or the tight, warm heat of her surrounding me. Together they bring my blood to a boil.

"Oh yes," she sighs. "I'll get used to you."

"All you need is practice." I reach down and rub my thumb against the top of her, igniting her own pleasure again. Blair's soft moans are the only sound as she begins to move, her hips sliding up and down on me. Her hair is a golden halo around her.

"You're not used to being ridden," she says, as if that's not a ludicrous statement, as if it doesn't send measures of unease and lust through me at the same time.

So that's what this is about?

She wants to be in control?

If she thinks this position is one where I'm at a disadvantage, she has it all wrong.

I reach up and cup her breasts. Her nipples immediately stand to attention, begging for my mouth. Rising up to suck her nipple into my mouth is simple enough.

So is tugging at her hair, kissing her skin, letting my hands run over the impossible softness of her. It's not long before she's down on her elbows and her hair is a curtain around us as I'm kissing her, holding her, my hips thrusting from beneath.

And when it's over, as pleasure spreads from my spine to my legs after my own release, she drapes herself over me. I wrap my arms around her and feel the beating of her heart, hearing the echo of my own in my ears.

"Well," she murmurs, "I think I'll enjoy this kind of practice."

I close my eyes and don't let myself consider what we've done, what this will lead to, how it'll inevitably end. The disappointment in Cole's eyes—the disappointment in *Blair's* eyes.

"Are you on birth control?" I ask instead. A question I should have asked earlier, but seeing as I was doing everything wrong, what was one more mistake?

Blair nods, rising to her elbows. Her cheeks are flushed.

"Good." I wince slightly as she shifts and I slip out of her heat. She stretches out beside me, her hand running along my stomach. I close my eyes and let her explore.

It's perilously close to cuddling, this, and even more of a bad idea than what we've just done. I'm still not strong enough to move away, the feeling of her soft hand on my skin like magic.

So I don't. I lie there instead, looking up at the ceiling and trying to catch my bearings. In two days, I have slept with her exactly twice, and I'm still no closer to being sated. If eight years of admiring her from afar had resulted in anything, it wouldn't be undone in a few bouts of passion.

But the facts remain.

She's my only friend's little sister.

She's not interested in anything long-term.

And I'm decidedly not the man likely to succeed in long-term.

I close my eyes, as if the darkness beckoning can chase those facts away. It doesn't, but her hand on my skin very nearly accomplishes the same thing.

"You've disappeared," she murmurs. I should move away. I should leave.

I can't bring myself to do either.

"I'm thinking."

"What about?"

I open my eyes. She's on her elbow beside me, the smile on her face sweet and kind and so much more than I deserve. She might not have a crush on me anymore, but I'll be damned if she gets hurt in any way because of this, because of me.

"About what way I'm going to give you your third orgasm," I say.

Her smile widens. "I'm sure you'll come up with something."

Gripping her around the waist, I pull her against me. How can a body be so supple, strong *and* soft at the same time? "Well, my favorite method is off-limits for now. I guess I'll just have to use my imagination."

Her laughter of delight as I flip us over banishes my negative thoughts entirely. There are some times in a man's life when he can't be anywhere but in the present, and at *present*, that's a pretty damn good place to be.

"I should get going."

"Okay." Blair stretches out on the bed beside me and watches as I get dressed. "You don't have to leave right away, you know."

"Yes, I do," I say wryly, "or you'll play twenty questions with me again."

"And is that so terrible?"

"Yes."

She laughs at my emphatic response. "Fine, be a mystery then."

"You like me like that." I drain the brandy in one gulp and then curse myself in the next. Now I can't drive home, and I'll have to send someone for the car. She has me so rattled it's hard to focus.

"I do," she says, coming up behind me and wrapping her

arms around my waist. I stand there for a moment, letting her hug me. "But I'll crack you eventually."

I break free from her hold and head to the door. "I'll see you at work tomorrow."

"Yes, you will." Blair leans against the couch, still completely nude, her crossed arms propping up her breasts. Does she know how the pose tempts me? Judging by the crooked smile she aims my way, she does, and it's deliberate.

"Go to bed," I tell her darkly.

"I will," she says. "But…"

"Yes?"

"You're coming tomorrow, right?"

I tug at the collar of my shirt. Tomorrow, when we have to spend yet another evening in the company of Cole and Skye. My nerves will be shot to hell after that experience—being around her brother now feels like lying. "Yes," I say, but not with any real excitement.

Her smile widens. "Good. Come over here first."

"Are you ordering me around now?"

"It's a suggestion," she offers. "But a good one. I take my practice very seriously, you know."

I shake my head at that, but there's no stopping the wry smile her words bring out. "I'll be here."

Seattle is quiet as I drive back to my apartment. The space looks different, somehow, seeing it with Blair's comments in mind. I suppose it is sparse. The living room has a giant TV for sports games. The couch doesn't have a single superfluous pillow.

Damn it. I'd never had difficulty finding female company. Not in my teenage years, not when I'd shot up like a weed and grown broad across the chest. Not in university, despite my poor grades and even poorer background. And not since I started making more money than I know what to do with.

But the women I go to bed with want me for my reputation. The name, the fame. They expect me to be dominant and harsh and big and strong. And for years, playing that role was enough. It was predictable. It was safe. It was shallow.

Blair is different. She'd *laughed* in bed with me tonight. Somehow, I was funny with her around. I go to bed with the scent of her hair still clinging to me and sleep deeper than I have in months. Funny how doing the wrong thing can feel so right.

When Cole had said that she used to have a crush on me…

The first thought was, *What have I done?* If this meant something to her—something real, something deep, something fragile —and I'd indulged in having her…

But she'd disavowed me of those illusions. She'd as good as admitted it was just one of Cole's jokes. Exactly what I wanted to hear—I couldn't in good conscience have followed her up if it'd been true. And yet, the first thing I'd felt when she said it hadn't been triumph.

It had been disappointment.

17

BLAIR

"Come here." The dark command in Nick's voice is impossible to resist. I cross the living room to him, my hairbrush still in hand, and surprise him by climbing into his lap, one knee on either side.

"Are you going to make us late?" I ask.

"To an event I didn't want to go to in the first place?" Nick reaches up and runs his fingers through my hair, undoing the hard work I'd just done with the large curling iron. "Yes."

"Cole and Skye asked us both," I point out.

"He asked me while I was half-dead, stumbling off the tennis court." Nick's eyes are locked on my neck as his thumb moves over my pulse. It quickens at his touch. "I'd near forgotten all about it until you reminded me yesterday."

"Are you that against opera?"

"Can you even be *against* the opera? It's not a cause you can champion."

"Of course it is. That's what Cole's doing tonight," I protest. My brother had donated generously to the Seattle Opera and was now rewarded with a private box on opening night. Although, knowing him, it had probably been for networking or business and not so much for a genuine love of the art.

"You blue bloods," Nick says dryly. "I should never have gotten involved with you."

I straighten the collar of his tux and enjoy the feel of his large body against mine, the touch casual and reassuring. My heart does a double-take when he presses a soft kiss to my cheek.

"Aren't you happy you gave *me* a chance? I'm not so awful when you get to know me."

He leans back against the couch and watches me through half-lidded eyes, large hands gripping my bare waist. My skin is still damp from the shower, dressed only in underwear.

"No," he says. "You're so much worse."

I laugh. "Yes, I am. And you spent years disliking me in vain."

"You thought I didn't like you?"

I raise an eyebrow. "In eight years, you've never once responded to any of my attempts at friendship. None of my invitations to events. No attempts at conversation."

Nick is quiet for a beat. His hands move instead, sending shivers across my skin as they trail my waist, my breasts, my shoulders. "It was simple self-preservation," he says quietly. "Not dislike at all."

My heart skips a beat.

The words hover on my tongue. *You know that crush I said was over? Well, I am over it—it's now full-blown infatuation.*

But I can't imagine anything that would make Nick run away from me faster. His lack of commitment is legendary.

"Self-preservation, huh."

"Yes." He leans forward and kisses my collarbone. "Which *you* should cultivate. If you want to make it to the opera in time, and if you are too tender, you should go get dressed before my self-restraint snaps completely."

"I'm too tender?"

His fingers smooth up my inner thigh. "We did a lot of practicing yesterday. Aren't you?"

I am, in fact, but admitting that… "Yes."

"Then up you go. Put on a dress."

But I don't. My heart swells instead and I press my lips to the strong column of his throat. His skin is warm and I speak the thought aloud. "How come you're always so warm?"

Big hands smooth over my back. "Go get dressed."

"Come on." I kiss my way up to his ear. "Tell me."

"Why I'm warm?" There's quiet amusement in his voice.

"Yes. I demand an explanation."

His hands skate down the length of my arms with the lightest of touches. "Why are you so soft? It makes no sense. Skin shouldn't be *that* soft. Can you answer me that?"

I shake my head, his hand coming up to cup my cheek. "Some things have no answer."

"Exactly."

I feel the faint scarring on the inside of his palm. Taking his hand in both of mine, I turn it gently palm-side up, looking at the faint raised marks.

Nick doesn't say anything.

"How did you get these scars?" I ask the question lightly, like the answer isn't important. Like I haven't been curious for eight years straight.

Nick's hand curls in mine. "It was a long time ago."

"I'm sorry for asking. I know you don't want to talk about... anything relating to yourself, really. But I figured, you saw me looking and it was probably clear that I wondered, and it felt ruder to *not* ask when you already know I'm thinking about it. You know?"

A faint curl to his lip. Damn man for smiling so rarely that when he does, it completely takes my breath away. "You don't talk this way to everyone."

"I don't?"

"Oh, you're forward with most people, I'll give you that. And chatty and breezy and all that. But this nervous sort of rambling? Only with me."

I put his hand back in my hair and, obediently, he runs his fingers through it. It buys me time, but only a little. We're closer to some truths that would be better left untouched.

"Perhaps I'm more nervous with you."

His hand stops only for a moment, before it continues its slow, sensual movement. "I see."

That's all he says. I focus on the buttons of his shirt instead, undoing them one at a time, rewarded by the sight of his chest. "Don't worry," I say. "I'm getting more and more used to you each time."

"And that's a good thing?"

I force lightness into my voice. "Isn't it? Where do you see this going, Nick?"

His hands continue down to grip my waist tightly. Despite the strong hold, I feel like I'm floating, waiting for the answer, for the words I know will come. Have I made myself too vulnerable? I know he's not a man I'll get to keep.

"I have no idea," he says finally. The bleakness in his voice brings out my own.

"Me neither," I murmur. "The only thing we know for certain is that it's supposed to stay a secret."

"Oh, yes." Nick's hands brace on either side of my waist. "And that we still have a lot of practicing to do."

I roll my hips over the clear evidence of what we need to *practice* on, and he groans. "Don't. I already said—we have to leave soon, you're sore, and there's not nearly enough time for a proper training session."

"I know." I press my lips to his cheek. He's not a man to easily accept tenderness, and now that he is, I'm having a very hard to time tearing myself away. "Help me choose a dress?"

"*No*," he says. "If I have to watch you zip and unzip, there is no way you're coming out of your closet unravished."

"Fine," I grumble. "Be that way." But I'm smiling at him the entire way back into my closet. The black, silken dress I'd picked out is draped over the back of a chair, the heels I'd chosen waiting next to them. The ridiculous grin on my face refuses to fade.

Yes, the infatuation is real, all right.

"Tell me something!" I call.

"What?"

I wiggle my hips to get into the dress. "What was your favorite subject in school?"

"No more twenty questions!"

"That's the last question." I lie, slipping my feet into the nude heels. One last look in the mirror tells me I've chosen correctly. The dress had been an expensive purchase, but it's made for occasions like this. Long and with an asymmetrical bodice, narrow in the waist before billowing out around my legs. My hair is half-up, half-down, blonde ringlets falling over the one bare shoulder.

"Fine." His voice is closer, teasing now. "Recess."

"That's not a subject. Can you do up my zipper?"

Nick appears in the door to my closet and motions for me to turn around. "Math, then."

"Math? That was my least favorite."

"I'm not surprised." His hands skate down my waist to pull me close, pressing a kiss to the top of my head. "You look gorgeous. Let's go."

"I hate that we have to take two cars," I say. The idea of the two of us walking in together, my arm on his, a pair... "Twice the environmental impact, you know."

Nick doesn't seem fazed by my words. His voice grows hard instead, and my vain hope that he'll say *screw it, let's go together* evaporates. "Well, do you want your brother to find out?"

"No."

"Then we'll take different cars." His voice softens as he holds the door open for me. "But I'll be sitting right next to you during the performance."

Opening night at the Seattle Opera is a beautiful thing. A string quartet plays in the spacious lobby, the notes rising to the glazed ceiling above. An attendant hands me a glass of champagne and points me to the East Wing. "Your brother is over there, miss."

141

"Thank you." It's an odd thing to be recognized so easily. It's been years now, and it's still not something I'm entirely used to. Cole's fame and my own interest in fashion has somehow made us, well, *notable*.

Nick's waiting with Cole and Skye, as he should be, leaving my place five minutes before me.

We staunchly ignore one another.

Skye is wearing a billowing dress that hides her faint baby bump. She looks gorgeous, and I tell her that, but she only laughs. "I do my best to keep up with the rest of you."

"You're more than keeping up!" I say.

"*Thank you,*" Cole breathes. "Will you believe it from Blair, if you don't from me?"

"You're very kind," Skye tells me with a wink. Then her eyes widen, looking from me to Nick. "Why, look at that. The two of you match."

I glance from Nick's all-black dinner jacket, including an inky pocket square, to my own dress in ebony silk. "I suppose we do," I say, not looking at Nick. I hope he doesn't realize it had been intentional on my part—a foolish fancy, perhaps.

Nick's voice drops into unexpected playfulness. "I told Blair that today was my day to wear black," he says to Skye. "She never listens."

We're among the first to be escorted to our seats. I'm faintly aware that other guests are looking at us, but the feeling of Nick walking beside me quickly overshadows that. It's hard to focus on anything else when he's near.

He was right, too—he does take the seat beside me.

And as darkness falls, as the orchestra begins to play and the performers leap onto stage, electricity builds.

I want to tease him about the way he has to fold his long legs in the enclosed space. Half my time is spent admiring the performance and the other half wondering if I dare reach out for his hand.

I don't. But I want it noted that it took a lot of self-discipline.

An attendant is waiting for us when intermission begins. The entire second floor has been transformed into a champagne bar and mingling area, and we have a table reserved.

"This is excellent," Cole says, observing the people gathered. No doubt he's seeing them as a smorgasbord of important people he can talk to. "Oh, look at that. The new architects for the New York Opera are here. I should go over and say hello..." He keeps Skye by his side as he strides over. I shake my head at him, but launch into mingling of my own.

I'm deep into a conversation with fashion editor Grace Moras about the performance when it hits me that I haven't seen Nick for a while. He hates things like this. Has he slipped out?

But when I spot him, I almost wish I hadn't.

The woman he's talking to is easy to recognize. Dark hair, purple dress, a hand resting on his arm. I've seen her before— she's one of the gossip journalists at the city newspaper.

And I know they've been involved before. *Hollow,* I think again. It's uncharitable of me, but I'd chalk her right up in the category of women who only want his money and reputation.

The glass in my hand grows tight with my grip.

"What do you think?"

I force my focus back to Grace, to this moment. "I'm really sorry, I thought I saw... forgive me. What did you say?"

Her smile is amused. "I said, what's next for you? What's new on the horizon?"

There's no explanation for why the words tumble out of my mouth. I haven't told anyone, but here I am, telling her.

"I'm planning a brand launch." So calmly, too.

Her eyebrows shoot high. "You are?"

"Yes. It's been in the works for a long time, and it's now in the final stages."

"Can you hint at anything? What is it about?"

I laugh, though it's a bit forced. "Oh, I can't say another word, not yet. But you'll be amongst the first to know, of course."

"I'm looking forward to that." She touches her glass to mine.

Had that been sarcasm in her voice? I shake the suspicion off as a product of my own insecurities.

I head back to the box early. Neither Skye nor Cole is anywhere to be seen, no doubt still working the floor.

"Hey."

A hand flies to my throat. "What are you doing here?"

"Waiting for you." Nick's hands find my waist easily in the darkness of our box. "You really do look gorgeous in that dress, you know."

My irritation *almost* melts away at his touch. But then I remember how he'd let her touch him, and my jealousy is as irrational as it's infuriating.

A hand tips my head back. "No questions for me?"

There's only one, and it's on the tip of my tongue. I bite it back. "Cole could come back any moment."

"He was talking to the mayor, last I saw. He won't return before the second bell, and the first hasn't rung yet."

My hand digs into the fabric of his sleeve, feeling the solid, firm muscle of his forearm beneath. *I won't ask, I won't ask.*

"Did you match our outfits on purpose?" he asks.

"Did you speak to your ex out there on purpose?"

His thumb rubs a small circle over my ribs. "*My ex?*"

"The woman in purple."

"Hmm. Riley." His voice is amused, damn him. "That was ages ago, and we were never in a relationship."

"Right," I murmur. "You don't do relationships."

"Are you jealous, Blair?"

I scoff, trying to regain some small portion of my dignity. "No."

"Yes, you are. And you were the one who said your old crush was gone." He turns us around, my back against the velvet-lined wall, his body large against mine. "Are you sure that was the truth?"

"I'm completely certain."

His head dips and his lips make contact with my neck, right

below my ear. He's not fighting fair. "Then why would it bother you?"

"Why did André bother you?" It takes effort to phrase the sentence, with Nick's lips trailing my exposed collarbone.

"You know the answer to that." His voice is a dark caress against my skin.

My eyes flutter closed when his lips find mine. They coax and press and tease, kissing me with expert precision. When he pulls away and rests his forehead against mine, my heart is a stampede in my chest. "Well," I murmur. "In that case, you already know the answer to your question. My crush never disappeared."

His breath catches.

There it is. He knows. My crush is more alive than it's ever been, humming between us, drawing me to him with every breath I take—strengthened by the kiss.

"Blair, I—"

The bell rings out, calling for the end of intermission. It drowns out whatever words might have followed. Nick steps back, and just in time, because the door to the box swings open a few seconds later.

The look in Nick's eyes stays with me for the rest of the show. It hadn't been one of happiness or triumph. No, he'd looked at me like I was a puzzle he couldn't understand, a prize he couldn't have, a treasure that just slipped further out of his grasp.

There had been no joy in those eyes.

18

BLAIR

Nick doesn't look at me for the entire second act. Part of me can explain that away—my brother is three feet away—but another part is silently begging him to just turn his head once.

As it turns out, silent begging usually falls on deaf ears. Who knew?

There's no hope of talking to him on our way out of the opera, either. And what would I say if there was? Take back the answer to his question? No—it's the truth.

We emerge out on the sidewalk after the performance, three chatty individuals and one very silent.

"That was *incredible*." Skye's eyes are wide, hands knotting the belt of her jacket. "I had no idea it would be so funny!"

"It's one of Donizetti's comedies, you know." Cole throws an arm around her shoulder. "One would hope it's funny."

She rolls her eyes at his teasing and turns to me for support. "Yes, well, I was just surprised that centuries' old humor still holds up."

I can't resist. "You read centuries' old books all the time."

Skye narrows her eyes and looks between us. "I think I like it better when you're not on the same team. Nick, help me out."

At her words, Nick turns his gaze back to us and the conversation at hand. "Whatever you need," he says.

Cole chuckles. "Man, you're not listening at all. Was the opera that bad for you, then?"

Nick's jaw tightens. "No, not at all."

"A love potion," Skye says with a sigh. "The ultimate plot device. It was a bad idea from the start."

"Well, Nemorino thought he didn't have a choice," I say, sympathetic for the main character's struggles with unrequited love.

"There's always a choice," Skye says. "He could simply have explained to her what he felt."

"As any self-respecting man would," my brother agrees. He tucks Skye in closer to his body. She responds in kind, glancing up at him. The quick look is filled with so much emotion that for the first time in ages I have to look away.

"We're going to head home," he says. "Charles should be here any second with the car. Who wants to be dropped off?"

Nick shakes his head. "Thanks, but I have plans."

"All right. Thanks for coming." Cole reaches out and gives Nick a slap on the shoulder. "See you on Thursday, right?"

"Yeah. You won't win this one, I'm telling you."

Cole's grin is wide. "Well in that case, I'm not listening. Blair? Going home?"

"Yes." Nick might be staying out, but I'm not. The night has been exciting enough as it is, and the last thing I want is to hang around in the hopes of being included in his late-night plans. Besides, it's not like we've defined anything, right? Going home is a good plan.

Apparently it wasn't.

No sooner have I closed the front door behind me than there's a furious knocking on it. Nick is there, his jaw working. "What was that?"

"What was what?"

He pushes his way into my apartment. "Going home, when I had a plan for us after."

I cross my arms over my chest. "How was I supposed to know that?"

"Because I said, *I have plans.*"

Dear God, save me from the idiocy of men. "And that was code somehow? When had we decided that?"

He tugs at the collar of his shirt and sinks down onto my couch. His arm drapes over a score of decorative pillows but for once, he doesn't scowl at them, keeping his gaze fixed on me. "So your crush never went away," he says.

"That's what this is about?"

His hand at his collar tugs sharply and the bowtie comes undone, the tails hanging down his chest. "Why didn't you tell me when I asked you the first time?"

"You mean after my brother made it into a joke?" I sit down on the arm of the sofa, wrapping my arms around myself. "Why do you think?"

"Damn it." He runs a hand over his hair.

"Does it matter that much?" I have to give it to my voice—it's deceptively calm.

"Yes. Because… if you're emotionally involved, I'm going to hurt you somehow. I always do." He leans his head against the back of the couch. "Fucking up relationships is what I do."

I lower my voice. "Why would you think that?"

The gaze he sends me is scathing, but it doesn't hurt. It's clear it's not me he's angry at. "History tends to repeat itself."

"It doesn't have to." I slide down onto the couch next to him. "And you know, you're not responsible for my emotions. Only I am."

His hand reaches out and lands on my knee. The silk of my dress has risen up and the scars on his palm tickle against my skin. "You say that *now*."

"And I'll say it again, even when it's painful. So I've admired you from afar for a long time." I shrug, even though I'm feeling anything but blasé. "So what?"

His thumb rubs a small circle on my skin. "So I don't want you to feel taken advantage of. That I offered something I don't know if I can live up to."

This is too much. I hitch my dress up and climb onto him, straddling him just like I had earlier this evening. Mere hours ago, perhaps, but it feels like a different night entirely.

"When did you get so morose?" I demand. "Trust me enough to let me look out for my own emotions and best interest, okay? And right now, I want to be with you."

His large hands come up to grip my waist. With his head still resting on the back of the couch, Nick's eyes are laden with intensity.

It's worth it. *Anything* that might come after this is worth it, just to be looked at like that by him.

"Say that last bit again," he says.

"I want to be with you?"

"Yes."

I smile. "Asking for praise, Nick. How unlike you. But okay." I press my lips to his cheek. "I want to be with you."

"Again." His hands find the hem of my dress and stroke up my outer thighs.

"I want to be with you."

A faint shiver runs through his body, so faint I almost think I've imagined it. He presses his lips to my neck. "And God help me, but I want you too."

I run my fingers over his scalp and he gives a low groan. "That's not a crime."

"Considering that your brother will kill me for it, yes, it is."

There's a million things I want to ask. Why does he think Cole will react so strongly? What parts of himself does he hide? But then his lips find mine and the thoughts float away, with nothing left to anchor them.

His kiss is different this time. It's deep, slow, tender. I kiss him back just the same, pouring out all the emotion I'd tried to hide from him before. *Yes*, I tell him with my lips. *I like you. Always have. Probably always will.*

His body shudders against mine when I take his hand and guide it to my breast. If it gives him permission or strength, I don't know, but a second later I'm lifted up against his body and carried slowly through my apartment.

Something tells me it'll be different this time. That the way our bodies yearn to be closer is deeper, that our conversation is still continuing, just with our touch as the language of choice.

Come here, I tell him with my hands on his shoulders. *Don't be afraid.*

I'm not, his mouth responds, kissing me so deeply there's no denying his passion. *I'm afraid* for *you.*

And when he strips the dress from me, when I lie there in nothing but my underwear and his dark gaze, I feel more comfortable than I ever have before. *Look at me,* I tell him, stretching my hands above my head and arching my back. *All yours.*

His hands are reverent when they touch the edge of my bra, searching around my back for the clasp. He teases the fabric off my skin and replaces it with his lips. They're warm and soft when they close around my nipple.

That such a simple thing can be felt so strongly is magic. It spreads through my body, through my torso, heat pooling in my stomach and lower still. I grip his head and lose myself in the sensation.

I'm dimly aware of his hands finding my panties, of them being tugged down my legs, of his mouth meeting mine again. "Let me go down on you," he murmurs, his fingers searching between my legs. I gasp as he presses down with the heel of his hand. "You can tell me to stop if you need me to. Anytime."

"Okay," I whisper, because there's no resistance left, and because being self-conscious around Nick is impossible. He chases all such thoughts away.

And when he settles between my legs... well, for the first time, I don't instinctively seek to close them. The skin of my thighs against his tanned shoulders excites me instead. So does his dark hair, his large hands finding my hips to hold me, not to pin, but to secure.

And when he puts his tongue to use... well, I close my eyes and surrender. I force the thoughts away, like I've tried to do so many times before, and amazingly... they obey. My self-conscious brain doesn't stand a chance against his strength.

His movements are slow, leisurely. So is his tongue. And for the few moments he lifts his mouth from me to speak, those words... they're like a balm across my skin. Compliments. About how good I taste, how he could do this forever, how he enjoys this.

We're still carrying on the conversation from earlier, all right. And perhaps this is his way of saying things he can't yet. I drink it in for what it is, and under his hands, I come apart.

It's slow, at first, the building of pleasure. So gradual I'm afraid of acknowledging it for fear it'll grow wings and fly away. But it doesn't. He grounds it, teasing my body, making himself at home between my legs. And when he uses his fingers to push inside of me at the same time as his tongue...

It surprises even me, the force of my orgasm. It sweeps through me with a power that leaves my back arched and limbs weak, forcing Nick to press down strongly against my hips.

Stay, is the message, even as my body is going and going and *keeps* going.

And I know then that whatever little crush I had on Nick is long gone. It's evolved into something much stronger entirely, something I would do anything to explore. The man between my legs, well... I've never felt for anyone the way he makes me feel.

He rests his head on my thigh and gives me a wide, open smile. "Well," he says. "Look at that."

I reach down and run my fingers over his cheek, over the dark stubble that always coats the lower half of his face. "I can't believe that happened."

"I can," he says, pressing a kiss to my skin. "And I was prepared to stay here for a lot longer than that."

"Did you mean what you said?" My question escapes before I can think it through. "While you were…"

His smile turns into something wholly masculine, pride and animalism combined. "Yes. Hell, yes."

"Good God."

He climbs up my body and I tug at his clothes, because how is he still clothed, and he laughs at my eagerness. It makes me even more eager—that he's here in bed with me and laughing with eyes that are lighter than I've ever seen.

He's so big, sprawled on my bed. The body of a fighter rather than a polished CEO. The animalism that always exudes from him, the one that's given him an edge in business, is graceful here.

I run a hand over his back and he turns, pulling me close, his hands ghosting over my skin. I lift my leg but he just slides his own under.

Reaching down, I grasp his hardness in my hand. It's still impressive, rock hard and velvety and impossibly girthy. It makes sense, I suppose. He's a larger-than-usual man. Why wouldn't that be reflected here?

"You're sore." He speaks through gritted teeth. "We don't need to practice every time, Blair."

"I want to," I murmur back. "Don't you?"

His laughter rumbles through his chest and into me, and as I stroke, he twitches in my hand. "What a question."

"We can go slow." My lips find his neck, and then I'm twisting, trying to get my leg over his hip so that we're better aligned.

Nick presses me close and flattens his hands against my back. The words he murmurs against my hair are half-muffled. "Women never want me to be gentle."

I frown, even as I pull him closer. What kind of women has he been with before? Riley, for one, who I'd seen today. The women I'd once generalized as only wanting his money. Perhaps they wanted his reputation, too. The idea of him—the vulture, the business tycoon, the man who destroyed businesses on a whim—didn't go hand in hand with soft sex.

His hands trace my spine with a tenderness that makes me want to break. "You can be gentle with me," I murmur.

And he is. He flips me over softly, settling between my legs, kissing my lips, my cheek, my neck. Reaching down, he guides himself in slowly, letting my body adjust to the size of him again. Both of us release the breaths we'd been holding when he's finally buried completely. His hands reach for my thighs, hooking them around his elbows, thrusting slowly. And when it's too much, he comes down on his elbows, his face against my neck.

It's deep and slow and sensual, and when he breaks apart, I wrap my legs around him as well as my arms. *Not going to let you go*, I think. *Not ever. Not now.*

I doubt I could.

If we're still communicating with our bodies, his is saying the same thing. It comforts me more than any of his words ever could.

When he rises up on his arms and pulls out of me with a soft wince, he doesn't disappear, either. He lies right next to me and pulls me into his side.

We don't speak for a long time, his hands tracing lazy patterns on my back. I rest my hand on his chest and enjoying the feeling of his hair through my fingers.

"You know," he says finally, "every woman asks about the scars on my palm. Every one. And I always tell them."

It takes effort to make my voice light, but I manage. "You didn't tell me when I asked earlier."

"No, I didn't. You're the first woman I didn't use them with."

"Use them?"

He sighs. "I got them when I was seventeen, and an absolute idiot. It was the last really bad fight I got into. I'd been asking for it, too, and antagonized the wrong guy. He pushed me through a window. I landed badly and had to brace myself on broken glass. Had to get stitches in both palms."

It's more than he's ever told me about his past. "That sounds painful," I say carefully.

"It was, a bit. My pride hurt more. I got a sound ass-kicking." He chuckles, but there's no humor in it. "And when women ask about it, well, I usually leave that part out. I just say that it's from fighting. And then..."

He doesn't need to continue. I understand—I can see the vision clear enough. They come to him seeking one thing, only knowing one thing about him, and he delivers. He gives them the narrative. Scarred palms, intense demeanor, rough sex. No relationships and no strings attached.

For a moment, I waver between pain and pity. I settle somewhere in the middle, reaching out to grasp his hand in mine. "And they don't want you to be gentle."

"No."

And perhaps there's more we don't say. *They don't actually want me,* he might add, were he a more talkative man. *They want the fiction.* I might have asked more, if I had been braver. But for now, this is enough.

I rise up on my elbow and trace a finger along his brow, down across a nose I now realize *must* have been broken at some point, over his lips and the rough cut of his jaw. "You said earlier that you stayed away from me out of self-preservation."

"I did," he says.

"I can't promise I won't hurt you, either. No one has that power. But... I don't want to. I don't want to come between you and Cole. I don't want anything we do to affect your business." My words run out, my mouth widening into a smile. "All I can say is that the time when you were my biggest source of irritation is long, long gone."

"Funny, that," he says, pulling me closer. "You're not so irritating anymore, either."

"No?"

"No." He kisses my still-smiling lips, silencing any further comment. I don't mind. Kissing is far preferable.

And for the first time, he spends the night.

19

NICK

Blair's hair takes up the better half of her pillow. In the low sunlight streaming in through her window, it's gold over white cotton, gleaming. One bare shoulder peeks out from underneath the cover. Despite the lateness of the season, her skin still carries the summer's tan.

She's breathtaking.

I turn my gaze away from her sleeping form to the overflowing walk-in-closet. The cacophony of colors and fabrics and sequins feels like an apt description of Blair herself. Overflowing with ideas and sparkle.

I run a hand through my hair. Spending the night at a woman's place. When had that happened last? I honestly can't recall—and this hadn't even been a conscious decision. I must have drifted off and then slept like the dead. It should leave me well-rested, but the idea is unsettling.

I feel disarmed.

Pushing back the covers, I walk out of her bedroom and into the colorful living room beyond.

Coffee. Phone. *Focus.*

I find a coffee machine in the kitchen and my phone in the pocket of my discarded jacket. There's a text waiting for me from Cole.

I push the phone away without looking at what he's written. The coffee washes some of the guilt away, but not all, the taste bitter and acidic.

He would not react well to this. The knowledge feels as obvious to me as my own name, as clear as the scars in my palm. Being with Blair would irrevocably change our friendship. Even if he grows to accept it—by some miracle of God—I'd always be the friend who went behind his back. Who didn't tell him straight up.

And if Blair ever had to choose between her brother and me...

Well. I take another sip of the scalding-hot coffee. I know where I'd end up in that equation. The path I'm on won't have a happy ending, and getting off it is the sensible choice, but I can't for the life of me imagine walking away from Blair now.

Not when the scent of her still clings to my skin and the sweetness of her words echoes in my mind. *I want you.*

Impossible? Try out of the damn question.

While she sleeps, I explore her apartment. The small knick-knacks she's collected. A framed picture of her and her late father skiing, his hand protectively on her shoulder. Skye and Cole's wedding picture is proudly placed in her bookshelf. I'm not surprised that she has that on display. The image of Blair with tear-glittering eyes comes back to me, her reaction to Skye's pregnancy.

I pause with my hand on a half-opened door. How had I not seen this before? Another guest room?

Shameless, relentless, I push it open.

I'm greeted by a veritable explosion of fabric, clothes, what looks like mood boards and charts... buried underneath it all is something that looks like a desk. The steel corner of an iMac peeks out behind a giant cardboard box.

Organized chaos, indeed.

I run my hand over the sleek, skimpy fabric on hangers and try to get a closer look at the pictures she's pinned to the wall. Above it all is a quote.

Work in silence, let success be your noise.

It makes me smile. Not in amusement, but in recognition of just how *Blair* it is. I can see her with her hair up, printing this out and pinning it up, determination on her features.

There's an audible intake of breath behind me. "Nick?"

Blair is standing in the doorway. She's wrapped a robe loosely around her waist. Any sleepiness in her gaze evaporates as she looks from me to my surroundings.

"Your office?"

"Yes." Her eyes keep darting to the lingerie on hangers, as if I've walked in on a crime scene.

I reach out and touch the silk carefully. "Something you'd rather keep under wraps?"

"Perhaps."

"All right." I run a finger over the lacy cup of a bra. "Although you're leaving me with a lot of possible options here. Do you work part-time as an amateur lingerie model or something?"

"No."

"Are you sure? There's an awful lot of it right here."

Just as I'd expected, her arms rise to cross over her chest. It's Blair's classic attack mode, one I've been on the receiving end of for years. I'm glad it's not lost entirely.

"Yes, I'm *sure*."

"If you're not going to tell me…"

She sighs. "I can't tell you, because then you might tell Cole."

Unease, at that. There are already too many things I'm forced to keep from him—Blair key amongst them. "What makes you think I would?"

Her teeth worry her lower lip. "Will you promise me you won't?"

For a split second, I consider saying no—avoiding deepening… *this,* between us. I'm on a balancing rope, tipping too much to the Blair side of the equation before wrenching myself back onto the Cole side.

But then I register the emotion in her eyes. *Trust.* She's

looking at me like she already knows my answer, and it's yes. My will crumbles like drywall under a sledgehammer.

"I promise," I vow.

She puts a hand on my arm and turns me around, pointing at a set of logos on the far end of the wall. "I'm starting another fashion company," she says carefully. "It'll be very different from last time. My name won't be anywhere on it."

Ah.

Her hesitations make sense, now. The backlash she received after the last time was enough to make anyone with less conviction pack up their bags and leave the industry all together.

Blair hadn't. She'd ridden out the ridicule and continued showing up to fashion events, dressed impeccably, and slowly restoring her influence as someone with taste.

Her eyes dart from the logos to mine. "I'll launch it without any connection to me. Until it has solid sales numbers, I won't be the face of it."

Yes, her hesitation definitely makes sense.

She releases me and hurries forward. "Remember these?" she says, fishing in a box for a pair of panties.

"Yes," I say darkly, "I do."

The ones she'd worn to the strip poker game in Whistler. The little beige flowers had haunted me.

"Well, I'll start off with lingerie. Made for all women, all shapes, all sizes, all colors. Flattering on the form. And then I'll move on to slips, functional bras, fashion tape, anything you might need to make your already existing wardrobe work better."

I reach out and run my hand over a packaging box with silk ribbons. It looks expensive. "Who are your investors?"

"I don't have any."

My eyes snap back to hers. "You're financing this yourself? All of it?"

"Yes." There's something in her eyes I can't quite name. Pride, certainly, but…

"It's risky as hell," I say honestly. "Why haven't you involved Cole in this?"

"Because I want people to respect it."

"People would."

She raises an eyebrow. "Would they? After last time? I don't think so. You didn't receive any help with starting your company," she points out. "Would you respect me if I did? Seattle certainly didn't last time I launched something."

Ah.

A suspicion grows. I walk around the room, looking at the piles of samples and packaging and mood boards. "How long have you been working on this?"

"A bit over two years."

"A bit?"

"More like three," she admits.

"Right."

She worries her lip again. When she speaks, I can tell she'd rather not have. "Tell me what you're thinking."

I reach out and put my hands on her shoulders. They feel frail under my hands, but I know they're not. She's stronger than she gives herself credit for.

Her eyes flick down to my chest. Right. I hadn't put on anything but my boxers.

"Have you ever kickboxed?" I ask her.

She bursts into surprised laughter. "No."

"Well, you're about to." Pulling her into her living room, I grab at the decorative pillows on her couch. I'll finally give them a purpose.

"What?"

"You've worked for three years on that in there and not told anyone?"

"I've told Skye."

"When?"

"Well… a few weeks ago," she admits.

"That's it," I say. "Bend your knees, sink into a fighting stance… yes, like that. Left foot forward."

Her face an adorable mix of confusion and resignation, she sinks into the stand I'm showing her. "Why are we doing this?"

"If you keep going at this rate, you'll launch sometime in 2029," I tell her. "You're afraid."

She straightens out of her fighting stance immediately. "I'm not afraid."

"Of course you are. Your first collection went down terribly. It couldn't *possibly* have gone any worse." I hold up two of her pillows as makeshift boxing pads. "Now hit me."

Blair looks from the brightly patterned pillow to my face, and back again, as if doubting which one she should truly hit. Only one of them has done nothing to her. "You've gone mad."

"No," I say, "you're just not mad *enough*."

She rolls her neck and bends her knees, just like I showed her. "Fine. I'll play along, but only because I've wanted to hit you so many times and never had the opportunity."

I smile at that. It widens as she punches, hitting the pillow with all the force of a mosquito.

"You can do that harder. You're strong, you know. You have strength in your shoulders and hips that you never use. Use it now."

Her gaze narrows with focus on the pillow I'm holding up. The punch she throws is harder this time. The flap of a hummingbird wing, perhaps. "That's it," I say. "Now, do all those gossip journalists make you angry? The ones who write that you have more money than fashion sense?"

Her eyes flash. For a second, I wonder if I've gone too far. These are words I know she's read. But sometimes there's a difference between knowing something and hearing it, especially from someone else's lips.

But then she punches again, her torso twisting, and the pillow reverberates from the blow. *"Yes,"* she says.

"And the so-called fashion experts who thought your first collection was…" I rack my brain to find a fitting adjective. Frankly, I'd seen nothing wrong with the clothes, the few ones I'd seen. What had they said? What's the jargon here?

Blair fills it in for me. "Derivative," she says, voice heated. "Disjointed. Passé."

And then she jabs. The form is off, but the power is there, as both of the pillows I hold up succumb to the incoming slaughter.

"That's it," I murmur. "Keep going."

She puts more vigor into it, and as I watch, she actually starts bouncing on her toes. "Twist from the torso," I instruct. "So what now? Are you going to let their opinions from years ago affect you, here and now?"

"No."

"I think you are. I think you're going to be too careful with this new launch."

"*I won't be.*" A flush creeps up her cheeks as she punches away, her breath coming faster. Her hair flows around her with every move and the robe is starting to come undone, tan skin peeking out. She looks like a vengeful, golden goddess. One with very ineffectual punches, perhaps, but a goddess regardless.

"They'll call it a comeback," she pants. "And even if they don't... I'm not doing it for them."

"That's it," I say. "Now use your legs."

She looks up at me. "How?"

I twist my hands to hold the pillows horizontally. "Hold on to my shoulders and raise your knee. Over and over... Yes, like that."

"Won't I hurt you?"

I scoff. "Only if you insult me like that again."

"What do you have against the pillows?" she says, but she does as I've instructed, raising her knee a couple of times in rapid succession. Without the pillows and my own vigilance, she'd have easily kneed me in the balls.

"They're useless," I say. "Frivolous and decorous."

She gives a twisting smile. "A lot of people would say the same about me."

"And what would you say to them?" Her smile turns wicked,

and then she's using my shoulders like a lever to pull her knee up even harder.

"That's it." I give her a gentle push and she stumbles back, eyes on mine. "Now jab. Hit me. Come on."

She does, and hit by hit, the tension in her face drains away. "I wish I could actually do this to all the critics."

"How violent of you."

Her smile is a glorious thing. Wide and true and tinged with just a hint of wickedness. "We all have hidden sides."

I sink down into my own fighter stance, still keeping the pillows held high. "Take it all out, then, so when you do face them, you're not angry anymore. You're indifferent."

"Is that why you fight?" she says, panting now.

Not where I want this conversation to go. I dodge her blow and question alike, sidestepping. "Can't keep up?"

She frowns and follows my parrying, trying to reach the pillows as I move them higher or sideways. *Stop moving.*

"Most targets don't stand still for you."

"You never do," she says. "These punches are for you, now."

"Oh?"

"For ignoring me for so many years." Punch, punch, punch. "For all the little comments." Punch, punch. "For making it clear to everyone, all the time, how much you disliked me."

I frown at her over the fringed hem of a pillow. She's still smiling, and her voice is teasing, but the words are true. They send another wave of guilt barreling through me. Throughout the years, I've always told myself that pushing her away was for the best. Not once had I really thought it through from her perspective.

One more deficiency to add to my ocean of flaws.

Blair reaches up for an uppercut but grimaces as her hand makes contact with the pillow. Dropping out of her stance, she clutches her fist to her chest, head bent. "Damn."

"What happened?" I drop the pillows. "Did you hurt yourself?"

That's when she strikes. Her not-so-injured-after-all hand

strikes out and collides with my upper arm. It only smarts for a moment. "Aha!"

Her grin fades as she sees my expression. I'm keeping it carefully blank, knowing that my dark stare usually unnerves people.

"Nick?"

I attack. I bend my head and wrap my arms around her waist. It's no effort at all to lift her up and throw her over my shoulder.

"Now you're in for it," I say.

Her laughter rains down my back, her hands gripping at my skin. "It was an accident!"

"Like hell it was." I throw her onto the couch and I'm on her a second later, tugging at the clasp of her robe. "This needs to go."

She gives me a blinding smile as she arches her back to let me slip it off her. "I'm not objecting," she says. "Naked boxing sounds so much more fun."

"When it's with you, yes." I pause with her beneath me, my hands on her waist. "Launch your business," I tell her. "When it's right. And tell Cole. He'll be overjoyed."

"I will, in time."

"Good." Bending down, I press my lips to hers. She sighs against my mouth and I surrender to her sweetness. What's a man to do, when confronted with this absolute goodness?

I'm kissing down her neck when the bell to her intercom rings. Someone's downstairs.

I groan. "Did you order food?"

"No." She presses a kiss to my cheek and slides out from underneath me. "Someone's probably calling the wrong apartment. It happens often."

"It does?" I watch shamelessly as she walks naked to the panel by her front door. Confidence now radiates from her.

"Yes," she says. "My neighbor's mother often visits. She's seventy-eight. Wrong buttons get pressed."

But when she presses down the *answer* button, the voice that rings out is alarmingly familiar to the both of us.

"Ready or not, I'm coming up, Lairy," Cole announces. "I have a surprise, and it can't wait."

20

BLAIR

I'm frozen by the intercom. There's no way I can refuse. No way at all, not convincingly. Illness? Wanting to sleep in? Cole won't accept any of those. I've barged into his home enough times that he'll want revenge.

"Blair?"

His voice propels me into action. "Come on up!" I chirp manically, pressing the button to let him in downstairs.

"What the hell?" Nick is bending down to grab pillows, throwing them haphazardly back on the couch. "Why did you let him in?"

"What else should I have done?" I grab my robe and pull it tightly around myself, double-knotting the belt. "He drove me home yesterday! He knows I'm here!"

"Fucking hell." Nick's face is the picture of quiet fury. He strides into my bedroom and snaps up his clothing, balling it against his chest. "I'll be in your study. Don't open the door."

"It locks from the inside," I say. "But… do you have to hide? We'll have to tell him eventually."

Nick pauses with one hand to the door of my study. His eyes tell me everything I need to know about his emotions on this score. "Never would be too soon," he says darkly, shutting the door behind him. A second later, I hear the sound of a lock turning.

Right.

Splendid.

The doorbell rings. "Hurry up!" Cole calls.

"I'm coming, I'm coming…" I open the front door. "What was the hurry? Is that—oh! Cole!"

He laughs at my expression and gives the floppy-haired puppy in his arms a little bounce. The dog looks from him to me, black eyes roaming. *"He* couldn't wait."

"Oh, he's *adorable*. Come in, come in."

Cole sets the small Golden Retriever puppy down on the center of my carpet, and he instantly starts sniffing around, tail wagging.

"You bought a puppy?" I can't keep the happiness out of my voice. Sitting down cross-legged on the carpet, I put my hands out for the dog to sniff. He instantly pounces, giving small, puppyish nips.

"It's a surprise for Skye. I just went to pick him up and I thought I'd stop here first. I figured you'd like that."

"You figured right. Oh, stop it, you." The last is to the puppy, who is now on his back and clawing at my hand. I pull it away only to return to his tummy, stroking the soft fur.

"He's beautiful."

"Eight weeks old," Cole says. "He was the runt of the litter. I think Skye will like him."

"I think she'll love him. But… have you spoken about this with her? Are you sure she'll be happy?" There's no bite behind my words. It's impossible to keep up any form of resolve in the face of a puppy, especially one so cute as this one. He's given up his attack on my hand and is now crawling into my lap instead, sniffing at my robe, my hair.

"She'll be convinced as soon as she sees him," Cole says. "She mentioned wanting company while she writes from home. The house is big, as is the property. Besides, we have staff that can help look after him if she's busy."

I smile into the soft fur. That's so like Cole—big gestures and zero thought behind it. It's a trait we share. "She'll love it."

Cole's answering grin is tinged with just a bit of relief. Perhaps I was the first test, then. "Why a Golden?" I ask.

"She saw one on the street once and said it was cute."

"That was your sole data point?"

"Yes. It's a good family dog, too."

We watch the puppy as he leaves us to explore. He laps around the living room table twice, sniffing at every nook and cranny.

"He's making me want to get a dog, too."

Cole chuckles. "Right, with your lifestyle?"

"You think I couldn't?"

"I think you'd have to get up earlier than ten in the morning if you do," he says, eyeing my robe.

"You could at least try to keep the judgement out of your tone," I tell him, but my voice isn't the least bit offended. This is my role in the family. Cole is the successful, responsible one. I'm the social butterfly. He swam for the school team in high school. I was on the prom planning committee.

"I'll try," he says. "Did you have fun yesterday?"

"Yes. The opera was beautiful, although I'm not sure how I felt about all the modern changes."

"Me neither," Cole says. "At least they took a risk with it."

"Classics are classics for a reason." I pat my hands on the carpet and the puppy looks up immediately. He stares at my hands with an obvious thought in mind. *A challenger?*

He pounces and we roughhouse a bit, Cole joining in. "He reminds me of Pratt."

I laugh. There's absolutely nothing about this little puppy that is reminiscent of the pug our mother had when we were teenagers. "No, he doesn't."

"They're both dogs," Cole points out. "But yeah, that's perhaps the only similarity."

"What did Skye say when you left this morning? She wasn't suspicious?"

"She thinks I'm swimming." His hand stills over the puppy's stomach, fingers scratching. "Blair, how has working with Nick been? Really?"

I smooth my fingers over the dog's soft ear. How soundproof is the door to my office?

"I've enjoyed it," I say. "We don't see each other a lot at work, actually. We sort of have a separation of church and state going on."

Cole nods, and when he speaks, his words are measured. "I asked him the same thing the other day, and he said that it had worked out all right but that he wouldn't renew your consulting contract. That it had run its course."

I'm grateful for the puppy between us, not to mention the door between Nick and me. My reaction is mine alone. "Oh? He did?"

"Yes. Surprised me, to be honest. I'd gotten the same impression as you. That working together had gone all right, at least on the professional front. You still can't seem to stand each other socially." His voice turns teasing. "Did you speak a word to each other last night?"

"Well, maybe he feels differently," I say. My voice is impressively casual. Someone nominate me for an Academy Award, stat.

Cole's voice softens. "I want you to find your passion again, you know. I thought maybe his company could help you with that."

Wow. What can I say in response? Even if I felt ready to show him my new brand, there's a six-foot-two beast of a man hiding in that room. One who happens to be Cole's best friend.

"I will," I say. "I'm doing an interview for the *Seattle Tribune* just next week about styling winter outfits." The response sounds weak, even to my own ears. For the first time, I almost *want* to tell him about my lingerie company. Had Nick's punching tactic worked?

"That's good to hear," Cole says. "You'll let me know if you need anything from me, right? I was the one who talked you into working for Nick in the first place. I can get you out of it if you want."

"Thank you." Keeping secrets from my brother isn't a common thing for me, not since we both grew up and out of the usual teenage tension between siblings.

What *would* he think about Nick and me?

The puppy gets to his paws and continues his exploration. When he gets to the closed door of my study, he whines slightly, pawing at the door.

I pick him up. "Perhaps you should get this little guy home to meet the rest of his new family."

"Perhaps I should." Cole accepts the wriggling puppy from my arms, tucking it into his. "Now, we have a ten-minute car drive. Can you handle that?"

The puppy licks his chin.

"That was a yes," I supply. "Now scram. And make sure you take a ton of pictures, okay? Of Skye's reaction, of the puppy settling in…"

"I will."

"And you know this means I'll be coming over to your house even more often."

Cole grins. "Timmy said the exact same thing. He's there now, in on the secret and keeping Skye company."

"I bet he's very excited."

"Oh, ecstatic." Cole lifts one of the puppy's paws in a tiny farewell before he closes my front door behind him.

Despite the information just revealed—the conversation I know is waiting behind me—I give myself a second to just smile. This would never have happened before my brother met his wife. He would have been working today, on a Saturday of all days, as he did most days. He would have scoffed at the idea of getting a dog.

How the times have changed.

Behind me, the door to my office swings open. Nick is fully dressed now. "Was there actually a *puppy* in here?"

"Yes. Cole bought him for Skye."

A hint of a smile on his lips. "Your brother is completely whipped."

"He's happy." I cross my arms over my chest. Nick won't distract me from my question, not even if he gives me one of his rare smiles. "He told me that you're not planning on renewing my contract. I thought my work with B.C. Adams was going well?"

He sighs. "Damn it. Thanks, Cole."

"So it's true? And you told him before me?"

"He asked. I answered." Nick shakes his head, looking away from me. "It's not a good idea for us to do… *this*, while we work together."

I blink. That was not the answer I'd been expecting. Hope, already blooming in my chest from the closeness we'd shared yesterday, grows with his words. "Oh. I totally understand that," I say. "Being involved and working together isn't a good idea."

"No, it's not." His eyes narrow a tad. "That was too damn close of a call with Cole. Does he swing by unannounced like that often?"

I wrap my arms around his waist. He looks out of sorts, like the close encounter had rattled him to his very bones. Someone else might think he looked imposing or closed off, but I see it for what it is now. He's uneasy.

"Sometimes," I say. "But isn't it fun to sneak around, at least for a little while?"

He reaches up and pushes back my hair. "That excites you?"

"A bit, but it'll feel much so better when he knows," I say, remembering the closeness we'd shared yesterday, the conversation without words. "And if you don't want me to work for you anymore, if you see this going somewhere… well, then it doesn't have to be a secret."

Softness had been the wrong tactic.

It breaks against him like a ship against an iceberg, unyielding and unforgivable. "Tell Cole and Skye," he repeats. The gentleness in his voice isn't the same as mine—his is cold. "And then what? Do you expect us to arrive to dinner at their house hand-in-hand and announce that we've decided *what*, exactly? To get to know one another better and please wish us luck?"

The scorn in his voice... Is that so unthinkable? "Why not?" To my horror, my voice wavers. "There's no rush, but yeah... one day, *eventually*, I do kind of hope we'd do that."

Nick shakes his head, pushing away from me gently. "I can't do that. I can't *be* that for you."

"Why not?" I hate the smallness of my voice, the meek question.

Nick pulls at the dark fabric of his coat. It stretches across his shoulders, struggling to contain an uncontainable man. I can empathize.

"Can't you imagine it?" he says. "What they'll say, what they'll think. It won't work."

"Nobody will care."

"Everybody will care," he says. "Have you never read the newspapers, Blair? You're admired far more than you're scorned."

"You think I care about what people might say about us? People I've never even met?"

"I know you would," he counters, throwing an arm out in the direction of my couch. "You just punched everyone who ever critiqued your business sense. What will you do when they critique who shares your bed? You think I don't know that everyone in your circle, your own mother included, wonders why your brother claims me as his friend?"

He's thought a lot more about this than I have.

I shake my head. "That won't happen. And if it does, I'll handle it. Just give me more pillows to punch."

"You say that now," Nick mutters, a hand on the handle of my front door.

"You're leaving?"

"I don't see us getting anywhere with this discussion right now," he says, and the tone in which he speaks... it's the same one I've heard him use for years. Cold, dismissive.

171

The door shuts behind him with a decisive sound. I sink down onto my couch with a sick feeling in my stomach. How had everything changed so quickly? Where, exactly, had the day gone wrong? I'd fallen asleep in his arms, closer to him than I'd ever been before, and now he's running as fast as he can.

A puppy would probably be easier to manage, I think, but I don't even have the energy to smile at the thin joke.

21

BLAIR

"Are you certain?" Gina asks, the professional concern in her eyes warming me.

"I am," I say. "I feel like I've done all I can to consult on B.C. Adams' new image and inventory. The rest is up to your financial team and marketing experts."

She nods reluctantly. Both of us know I'm making sense. "I understand that, and I can imagine that you have a lot of projects competing for your time. It's a shame, though. You have a keen understanding of this industry and I'll be the first to recommend that we bring you back if we have need of it."

Is it possible to grow a few feet from praise alone? I feel like I have. "Thank you, I truly appreciate it. Would you mind informing Mr. Park about my letter of resignation during your afternoon meeting?"

"Not at all." Faint speculation is in her eyes. "I was under the impression that you were family friends, though."

"Oh, we are, but he's nothing if not busy. I'll call him tonight and explain."

She taps her fingers against my desk. "Very well, then. Feel free to leave your keys and access pass here when you leave."

I release a shaky sigh as she walks away.

This is the right thing to do. I accepted this job to prove a point to Nick and Cole, and the point has been made. B.C. Adams' profit margins are getting better by the day.

I leave the office without having glimpsed Nick once that day. Professionalism to the very end, I think, gathering up my few belongings and waving goodbye to his assistant. The decision feels like one of those punches that Nick wanted me to throw in my living room. He goes after what he wants, and so would I.

And if he believed we couldn't work together and still be involved, I've just made it really, really simple. I'd rather have *him* than this job.

———

But he doesn't pick up when I call to tell him that.

He doesn't pick up the day after, either. My two texts—one polite, one mildly frustrated—go unanswered. Is he still upset from when he'd stormed out of my apartment?

It's hard to ignore the feeling that you're a fool. It creeps up when you least expect it, resistant to common sense and rationality. We'd had one little fight. Hardly even a quarrel. Practically a disagreement. *A discussion.* And then he'd run?

It didn't seem like the Nick I'd gotten to know, the man who steered his company with an iron grip, who was competitive to a fault, who was proud and private and shockingly loyal.

But it did seem like the actions of a man who had a decade's experience of keeping women at arm's length. And that thought made me feel more foolish than any other. That I'd had the arrogance to think *I'd* be the one to make him change.

On the fourth day post Puppygeddon, as I was beginning to think of it, I ask Cole to come over to my apartment. With no work and no Nick, there has been nothing to distract me from my own business plans.

And it's time to throw another one of those punches.

"What's this?" Cole asks, standing on the threshold to my

office. "I didn't even know this room existed—you've kept it closed for years. It's not a spare closet?"

"Nope. I've been working on something." I'm standing by the rack of clothing, nerves racing through me. I feel like I'm seven again and asking him to play with me, scared he'll say no.

Cole steps inside. The change when he starts to realize what he's seeing is instantaneous. His face grows sharp, his business persona, the one I've seen him adopt a thousand times. "Blair, what is this?"

So I tell him. I lay out the entire launch schedule I've plotted out over the last couple of days. I show him pieces and sketches. Packaging design. I even hand him the spreadsheet of my financial calculations.

My brother reads it all—every word, every cent, every thing he's shown. The quiet concentration on his face is the greatest compliment he could pay me, even if he hasn't commented yet.

And then the questions start. *Where do you store your stock? Who's your distributor? What's the long-term vision?*

I answer all of it to the best of my ability, and when I'm done, he sinks into my office chair. "Well," he says. "I'm very impressed, Blair."

"You are?"

"Yes. You've mapped it all out meticulously. There are some areas where I think you should hire outside expertise, but overall... you're set." He raises an eyebrow at me. "I'm hurt, actually."

"Hurt?"

"You must have investors already, but it's the first time *I'm* hearing about this. My money not good enough?"

I shake my head. "No investors."

"How are you paying for all this?" And then, his narrowed eyes. "Your inheritance?"

If I speak quickly, perhaps I can pre-empt his anger. "I wanted to do it on my own. If this doesn't work out, if it's not a success... I couldn't have you or someone else take the financial hit again."

Great. Now he looks offended. "You thought I wouldn't help you?"

"I knew you would. Cole, I'd love for you to invest, truly. *After* I've launched—and only if you look through the financials with your advisors and make a decision on the basis of that."

He's quiet for a beat. And when he speaks, there's something in his voice—respect? "I get it."

"You do?"

"Of course. It's risky as hell, but yes. Dad and I once had this exact same conversation." Cole smiles at the memory. "I'll help you in any way I can—as much as you'll let me."

"Thank you."

"Start by getting an assistant and a centralized storage location," he says, softly shaking his head. "Two years, and not a word to me. It'll take me a while to forgive you, you know."

His voice is teasing, so I make mine light as well. "I'll do your chores for a whole week."

It works—he laughs. "Make it two."

We talk about the puppy, still nameless and too cute for this world. About Skye's upcoming book and Cole's trip to New York. So I convince myself it's casual, when I slip in the question toward the end. "Have you seen Nick around lately? He's sort of been MIA since the night at the opera."

"I haven't. He cancelled tennis yesterday, but that happens all the time. Busy schedules and all. Why?"

Why, indeed? I clear my throat. "Just wondering."

"He hasn't been at work?"

No, I haven't. I should tell him I've quit, but then I'd have to explain why, and... I can't.

"Not really."

"He'll be at the party on Saturday, anyway," Cole says, not the least bit concerned. It's only been a few days for him, after all, and the two of them haven't had a massive argument. Nick had obviously been able to text Cole, but not me.

So his phone works.

Good to know.

I file it away under the *reasons to get angry* column instead of the *reasons to get sad* one. It's been a constant battle this past few days between them both. As the ruling judge, I've made an executive decision to give him at least a week. But if he's still avoiding me by Cole and Skye's party...

All hell will break loose.

So, I have to break hell loose.

It had seemed a lot easier earlier in the week. But standing in front of the floor-length mirror in my bedroom now, getting ready for a party he will most definitely be at, it's much harder to keep my confidence up.

An entire week where he hasn't answered my calls.

But tonight he won't get away.

The dress I'm wearing clings to my form. The colors are appropriate—Skye sent me a picture of the autumnal decorations—in muted tones. I'm wearing my own lingerie underneath. It feels like lace armor, like I'm preparing for battle.

Cole and Skye's driveway is decorated with pumpkins and flowers and a giant wreath hangs on the door. A member of staff with an orange maple leaf in his breast pocket opens the front door for me.

"Thank you." The scent of pumpkin spice hits me. Are they burning a legion of candles at once? Baking cookies nonstop? The place smells amazing.

Skye is the first to find me. She threads her arm under mine. "Isn't this place gorgeous?"

"It's your place," I point out, laughing. "But yes. Are you making this an annual tradition?"

"I really want to. Of all of Cole's damnable networking parties, this one I want to keep. And make it more about family." Her hand flutters absently to her belly, now really starting to show. No doubt she's already fielding off questions.

"Next year you'll be three hosts," I whisper.

Her gaze warms. "Yes. I'm sure the third will be a huge help."

"Infants are excellent napkin-folders," I tease.

Skye laughs, tugging us to a standstill in the center of the living room. Soft music drifts from the built-in speaker system. My eyes pass over the people gathered in this room. Family friends. My cousins. My brother and Ethan Carter, heads bent in close conversation. He's another one of Cole's recent friends—a man with a budding tech empire and two cute, tiny daughters. I've heard Skye say more than once that she hoped he'd find someone to date amongst the guests at their parties.

I don't see Nick anywhere.

"Your mom is in the kitchen," Skye says, misunderstanding my perusal. "She told Cole that she doesn't trust the new caterers to get the food quite right."

I smile at that. "Sounds like Mom."

Skye is polite enough to neither agree nor disagree with that statement, but I can't imagine that my mom makes for an easy mother-in-law.

"So," I say, looking down at my nails, "is Nick here?"

"Yes, I saw him just a few minutes ago. He was—oh no." Her gaze snags on the bar, where her teenage nephew is examining a few bottles. "I'll be right back…"

I head into the den. More people are here; the double doors open up to the backyard. Space heaters are set up outside and lounge chairs have blankets thrown over the backs.

Nick is standing out there. It might be dimly lit, but I'd know those shoulders anywhere. It's him—standing alone and apart from the rest of the party. It makes me a tiny bit less angry at him for having ignored me for a week.

I'm nearly by the doors when I'm stopped by a smiling face.

"Blair, it's good to see you again."

"You too, Uncle." I return his hug. *So close—I'm so close!*

He sees my gaze and follows it out to Nick. "Yes," my uncle says. "Your brother invited the vulture. He's always had a penchant for making news, our Cole."

178

My teeth grit together. At the reference to Nick's reputation in business. To the joke about Cole's public relations skills. To the fact that my uncle expects me to laugh to it.

A year ago, I probably would have.

"They're good friends," I say.

"Oh, of course they are." My uncle's voice quiets. Big words, but he wouldn't want to be overheard.

There's more I could say. About Nick's business sense, about saving companies rather than destroying them. Perhaps some ridiculous metaphor about how even vultures have a place in nature. That I've been working for him. Nick had once said that he didn't want to harm my reputation, somehow. And here I am wanting to defend his.

But I'm a woman on a mission, and correcting my uncle will have to wait. I look from him to Nick beyond. He's outside, in the dark and cold, choosing it over the warmth and commotion inside.

He always chooses to stand apart.

"Excuse me," I tell my uncle, and step out to join Nick in the cold autumn air.

22

BLAIR

"Here you are," I say, wrapping my arms around myself.

Nick doesn't look down at me. He keeps staring out into the distance, and even in the dim light, I can tell his jaw is clenched. "Found me," he says.

I swallow. "Why have you been avoiding my calls all week?"

"Why do you think?" He takes a sip out of a glass I hadn't seen him holding.

I glance back to the crowded room inside. We can't do this here—not with people watching. "Come on," I tell him. "Let's go inside."

And to my surprise... he follows without protest. I lead him around the back porch to the kitchen entrance. It's open, thank God, and none of the waiters raise an eyebrow as we walk through the butler's pantry to the back staircase. Nor do we run into my mother, and for that alone, I need to write a thank-you note to fate.

"Far away from prying eyes," Nick comments, but his voice isn't amused so much as it's dry. It's the Nick from months ago—the Nick who couldn't look at me with anything but disdain or indifference.

I thought we had banished *that* Nick forever.

"In here," I tell him, pulling him into my brother's study. It's the one room I can always count on being deserted.

Nick glances around. "This room. Again."

The room where we'd kissed. Yes, I remember, but I won't be sidetracked. Not even by the way his suit—worn disdainfully, as always—looks like it's cut specifically for him. The five-o'-clock shadow on his face is more pronounced, like he hasn't shaved in days, bringing out the heat in his eyes.

"So you finally have me here," he says. "Let's hear what you've wanted to tell me all week."

The faint hope I'd harbored falls with his words. Hope that there had been some form of misunderstanding, that he'd changed his mind, that the argument we'd had was truly no more than a bump in the road.

"That's your attitude?" My voice comes out more pained than I want it to. I brace my hands behind me against the desk.

"My attitude?" He raises an eyebrow. "You were the one who quit your job immediately after our argument, and without a word of explanation. Actually, let me go first, to spare you the trouble. You're right. This isn't a good idea."

My chest feels like it's caving in. "Working together?"

"Working together, getting to know one another, sleeping together." The seething force of his reply catches me off guard.

"That's what you want, then? For us to stop… what we've been doing."

His eyes are black and dazzling with unrestrained fury. Why is he so angry? I don't understand it. "Yes. That's for the best, isn't it? What you want and what I want isn't compatible."

"Right," I agree faintly.

"And now we don't have to talk to Cole about it." He rolls his neck, like it's stiff, glancing away from me. "Problem solved."

My words aren't considered. They aren't measured, tactical, precise. They flow out of me faster than I can dam them. "You're afraid again. You're afraid this might become something real, for once, so you're retreating."

"*I'm* the one retreating? You're the one who quit the job without a word. Whatever. I'm done with this. Go back to hating me, Blair. It was better that way."

And then he does the unthinkable.

He turns away, like we're done with this conversation, like this is all we needed to say. My hands tremble with anger as I cross the room to him.

"I quit the job *for* you, you idiot," I say. I grip the lapels of his jacket and pull myself up on my tiptoes. There's a glimpse of his face, set in angry lines, before I close my eyes and press my lips to his.

So we're not good with words.

But I'd like to see him lie with his lips.

His mouth is furious under mine, echoing the same anger in my own. His hands grip my hips and I'm pulled roughly against the full length of his body.

Yes, I think. You don't want to go back to being nothing at all. I know you don't. *Stop* being afraid.

Nick's hand rises up to bury itself in my hair and then he's fighting me for control of the kiss, his lips opening mine, his tongue sweeping in.

I surrender to his lead and slide my hands inside his suit jacket, along the hard planes of his chest, warm to the touch even through his shirt.

The sound of the door opening breaks us apart.

And standing there, shock on his face, is Cole, and behind him, a very curious Ethan.

To his credit, my brother doesn't scream or yell. He doesn't flip out. He goes very white instead.

"What," he says softly, "the hell is going on here?"

Nick steps away from me. A glance at his face tells me he'll be absolutely no help here. If Cole is shocked, Nick looks struck. The blacks of his eyes are flat.

"Cole," I ask, "please. Please, just give us a moment…"

He tears his gaze away from his best friend to me. And whatever he sees in my eyes is enough, apparently, because he reaches out and shuts the door to his study. The door slams behind him.

The room is drenched in silence.

Nick bends over Cole's desk, his hands braced along the edge. He looks frozen in place—a marble statue of misery. Atlas punished, I think. Prometheus bound.

The tension is clear in every line of his body.

"He'll understand," I say. "He will. There's nothing to—"

"He won't. Please, Blair. Tell him whatever you like, but just… leave me alone."

I don't understand his emotions. There's no clear path for me to approach them, no way forward, no obvious entry point. I take a careful step closer.

"Why do you do that? Why do you push everyone away?" I ask. And then stronger, when there's no answer. "It's easier to be an asshole than to have someone know you and walk away, right? Better to never give them a reason to get close in the first place."

His shoulders heave with one strong breath. "Go back to your friends, Blair," he says quietly. "We're done here."

The same words he spoke to me at the poker game, all those years ago. Tears prick at my eyes. What have I done that's so horrible? Caring about him?

I wish I didn't, so I didn't have to feel this way right now. Glad he can't see my face, I turn around and walk out of the study.

The door doesn't slam behind me. That would take more anger than I have at the moment. It closes with a soft creak, like a whimper, the sound echoing in my head as I race down the hallway.

23

NICK

The knock on my front door is heavy. If it hadn't been made from steel, it would probably bear marks.

"*Nick!*"

The voice is familiar. The fury in it is not. I run a hand over my face and contemplate not opening. Running from my problems has always been a much, much nicer option.

But it's also a short-term solution.

So I open the front door. Cole bursts through, the look in his eyes worse than a punch to the gut. Physical violence would have been *preferable* to that look. I'd left his party without seeing him, not wanting to throw a scene at his cozy, family-filled gathering.

But I'd known he'd come and find me soon enough.

"How could you?" he spits. "My sister?"

There are no words I can say to make it better.

None at all.

"I know," I say.

"Her explanation didn't make sense," he grinds out. "So maybe you can explain it to me? Because right now it's looking really fucking bad."

The image of Blair, upset and confused, trying to explain *us* to her brother explodes in my mind. And all because I hadn't answered her calls out of a fear that she'd tell me we were over. That she quit the job and planned to cut me out of her life.

"I don't know if I can," I say. Without conscious thought, I take in his stance, his closed fists. My legs brace against a sudden attack.

"*Try,*" he growls. "Because all I know is what I saw, and that a few hours later, my little sister is sobbing in my living room because of you."

Sobbing?

Blair was crying, about me? Because of me? The ground seems to tremble beneath my feet. "Is she okay?"

Cole turns venomous eyes on me. "I don't know, why don't you tell me?"

Fuck.

How do I even begin to explain this? When I'd considered having this conversation, I'd expected to have weeks to prepare myself. To find the right words to make Cole understand that it hadn't really been a choice at all.

I brace my hands against the back of my couch. "I didn't mean for it to happen."

"Oh, that makes it so much better," Cole says. "That you hurt my sister on a whim."

"It wasn't like that," I say, gritting my teeth. "Not at all. We grew closer. It wasn't planned, and I knew I should have stayed away, but…"

The look Cole shoots me is deadly. *Spare me the gory details*, it says, *or I'll kill you where you stand.* And I'd probably let him, because knowing Blair is somewhere crying because of me…

"But what? There are *thousands* of women in Seattle who'd have you. Fuck, I've seen you have your pick of them! But you had to choose my sister?" Cole's voice is vibrating with anger. "You were the one who told me to avoid mixing business and pleasure when I started dating Skye. *Don't make a mess*, was your advice."

Oh, the irony.

"It wasn't like that. It was never… never for lack of someone else. I didn't *want* another woman but her." My voice is hoarse. All our years together and we've never had a conversation like this. Never ventured into this territory. But just like when I'm with Blair, it all comes pouring out. "Damn it, Cole, you're basically my brother."

He braces his hands on the other side of the sofa. It's like a divider, the two of us boxers on either end of a cushioned ring. His shoulders are tense. He'd much rather punch me in the face, but he's resisting it. For now.

"I've seen you with women," he grounds out. "It's never emotional. It never lasts. It's always transactional in some way. Are you telling me that this is somehow different? That it's not just..." His skin goes dark red and I know the word he's not saying, the word he can't bring himself to. My reply is quick to save us both the pain of that.

"It wasn't for me. Never was."

And that's the truth of it.

For all the years I've stayed away from Blair Porter, it's been exactly for this reason. Crossing the line would never be unemotional. Never casual. It would be *something* right away—she would deserve nothing less. Hell, she'd *demand* nothing less. And she hadn't.

And I'd reacted like I knew I would.

"Then why is she crying? Why does she think it's over? Put the pieces together for me."

"Because it is," I say. "It's not... fuck, Cole, I don't know what to tell you. I'm not good at relationships. I'll hurt her. It's better that we stop it now, before it goes too far."

"Beautiful timing," he says. "Because I'd wager she's already pretty damned hurt."

His words feel like a slap. One I know I deserve. Had this been a kickboxing ring, I would have known how to respond. This, though... I'm drowning.

"She's strong," I say. "She's had to be. There's so much in store for her... I can't ruin any of it. Can't be attached to her name and jeopardize it."

"So much in store for her…" Cole echoes, eyes narrowing. "Do you know about the things in her home office?"

"She told you?"

His eyes are twin flames of accusation. "*She* told *you?*"

A burst of pride erupts inside me. She'd faced one of her fears, then, by telling him.

"She was worried about your reaction," I say. The words slip out before I can stop them, a testament to how unhinged I'm becoming.

It's the wrong thing to say. Cole's eyes blaze. "*She told you that?*"

"Yes."

I can see the instant he realizes that he's miscalculated somehow. That there's more to the story here than he'd assumed, that this is both deeper and wider and broader. "Fucking hell, man. You've made such a mess of this."

"I know," I say. "It's over now, though. I'll leave her alone from now on. I *promise* you I will."

Cole shakes his head. "I'm so tempted to hit you right now. You're being even more thick-headed than usual. Would you give up this easily if it was a company you wanted to take over, huh? Would you give a fuck if your reputation wouldn't become attached to hers?"

I'm shaking my head too, this time in disbelief. "You can't possibly *want* me to continue seeing Blair."

"Don't tell me what I feel." Cole's fists tighten at his sides. "God help me, no, I don't *want* that. I've always said you needed a proper relationship in your life, but I never expected you to choose my sister for that."

I reach up to run a hand over the back of my neck. "I'm not sure I really *chose* anything," I mutter.

Surprisingly, Cole's lips twitch. "I remember the feeling," he says. "I can't believe I'm talking you into this. But for some godforsaken reason, my sister wants you. And I want her to be happy. And even though I'm furious at you right now, I want *you* to be happy. So fix it, Nick."

The order rankles me. He can see that it does, and the smile blossoms into a full one, savagely amused. Part of his revenge. "Do it," he says.

I don't know how to respond.

"You didn't react like I expected you to," I say. I'm pushing my luck by pointing this out, but that seems to have become a habit by now.

"Yes, well, don't give me a reason to change my mind." Cole shakes his head, stepping toward the door. "Make it right for both of your sakes. And for mine, because I'm forced to spend time with both of you."

And then he's leaving, and I'm alone with his words and my own thoughts, spiraling in every which way. And beneath it, a deep, yawning fear that I've pushed Blair too far this time. That had been my goal, after all. Push her away to avoid disappointing her. Stop this all from spinning out of control.

But I'd never had control when it came to her.

And maybe... maybe that wasn't such a terrifying thing. Maybe it might even lead to something good, if I was brave enough to try.

24

BLAIR

Nick and Cole aren't talking.

Skye informs me about it over brunch, a week after the horrible fall party and the showdown in my brother's study. She tells me while Cole's busy letting the puppy out into the garden to play, and with a careful glance in his direction.

That look tells me more than her words ever could. So whatever discussion they'd had hadn't gone down well.

I look down at my buttery croissant and swallow a rising tide of despair. Cole and Nick are unlikely friends, but they're true ones. Both of them need each other. Competitive and type-As and hard-working.

And I've come in between them, and for what? Nick and I aren't anything now. We're just two people who once used to spend time together. We were never even friends, not really.

"Oh, Blair, I'm sorry." Skye's hand lands on top of mine. "I shouldn't have said anything."

"No, I'm glad you did," I reassure her. "I want to know. Even if..."

Even if it hurts.

Skye nods, her eyes more understanding than I have any right to. It's my mess, this. Play with fire and you get burned. Hadn't I always known that in regards to Nicholas Park? And still, I'd poked and prodded, ignoring his attempts to distance himself. Was this what he feared? That he'd lose his best friend?

And I'd made it come true.

Cole returns to the table. His cable-knit sweater is frayed at the collar, and I make a mental note to buy him a new one for Christmas. "Strike is out," he says. "He's more obedient by the day."

"Because you're the one training him," Skye notes. "I'm not half as good at that."

"It's because you're not consistent." Cole drapes an arm around the back of her chair.

"Strike? You named him?"

"Timmy did," Cole explains. "We went over a list of baseball terms and settled on Strike."

"It suits him," I say. Next mental note: get them a collar with Strike's name emblazoned on it. I'm a Christmas gift queen.

Cole raises a finger at me. "Now, you told me you had more information about your company. Will you finally tell me the launch plan?"

I look through my bag for the papers I'd printed. It's massive, what I've planned. A tight time schedule. It'll be like throwing myself out of a plane window without knowing if the parachute works. But that's business, right? Not to mention life. You can stay at home, hiding under the blankets, but that's not what you were put on this Earth to do.

"Here it is." I push the timeline over the table. "I've planned the launch for February next year. Promotional packages will be sent out to a range of influencers and YouTube personalities. I'll pull every favor I can to build hype about it."

"And you've hired the marketing consultant I suggested?"

"Yes. She starts next week."

Cole sinks into the papers like I've given him the unreleased script to a Hollywood blockbuster. His interest and support for this makes my chest warm. Why had I been afraid to share this with him for years? Cole hadn't been an overnight success, either. My brother has worked for everything he has, and so will I.

A small part of me wants to hear Nick's thoughts on this. His business sense is acute, especially knowing when to cut your losses and run. What would he say?

I push the thought away.

Nick doesn't want to be in my life. *It's better if you go back to hating me, Blair.*

Well, I'd be damned if I'd let him get his way there, too. For all of my sadness... I refuse to hate him. I doubt I ever really did.

I come home to a giant package outside my front door.

And by giant, I mean *massive*. Cardboard and heavy packing tape. It can't possibly be for me—I haven't ordered anything—but the name on the package is mine.

I wrestle the giant package into my living room. I'm sweating by the time I finally grab a pair of scissors from the kitchen and begin opening it.

To find the giant thing surrounded in bubble wrap.

"Is this a joke?"

No one answers, of course, as I put the scissors to merciless use. By the time I have the thing uncovered, my living-room floor looks like World War Three has taken place and it was exclusively fought in packaging materials.

I take a step back to inspect it.

It's the quote from my study, the one I have printed up and taped to the wall above my desk. *Work in silence, let success be your noise.*

But it's carved into beautiful wood, the finishing smooth and polished, the letters highlighted with color. It's gorgeous.

Had he known it would arrive today, right as I'd come home from going through my company's launch plan? I look through my purse in search of my phone, to call Cole and say thank you. That he'd remembered and thought about this.

It's beyond thoughtful.

The buzzer of my intercom rings, but I'm not expecting anyone. Hesitantly, I press down the button to answer. "Hello?"

"Did you get my gift?"

It's not Cole's voice on the other line, not even Skye's. It's Nick's.

Even mangled through the bad reception of the intercom, the gravelly texture of it raises goose bumps on my arms.

"Blair?"

"Yes. It just arrived."

"Good." A pause. "Can I come up?"

I look around my space, at the packaging, the clothes on the back of the couch. At my own lackluster outfit.

"Yes." There's really no other possible answer to that question.

I know exactly how long it takes a person to get from the bottom of my building to the top, if the elevator is there waiting for them. It's about seventeen seconds.

Seventeen seconds to look myself in the mirror and realize that I need to run a brush through my hair. I apply Chapstick while I'm at it, shoving the hamper with dirty laundry into the corner of the bathroom, and shutting the door firmly to my office.

That's all I have time for, because then there's a knock on my front door and there he is. It's only been a week, and still, the sheer size of him hits me again. Tall and broad and intimidating.

Nick doesn't speak. He just looks at the giant quote, unveiled on my living-room floor, his hands flexing at his sides.

"I didn't think it'd be that big," he says finally.

I wrap my arms around myself. "It's lovely."

He nods. "How have you been?"

"Since we last spoke?" It's a stupid question, because what else would he mean, but it slips out anyway, perhaps in lieu of the roughly four thousand other questions I want to ask. *Why did you push me away? Why are you here? Why haven't you called?*

"Yes."

"Good. I've been working." I look away from his face to the quote on the floor. It seems like it's easier to face for the both of us than each other. "I've heard that you and Cole aren't really speaking."

A twist of his mouth. "No, not really."

"I'm sorry about that. That what we did affected your friendship. I never meant it to."

He shakes his head. "That's not something you should apologize for."

"No?"

"Blair, I..." He turns to me, running a hand over his hair. "What I said to you last time, in the office..."

"Yes?"

He shakes his head again. "I was afraid," he says. "Why is that so hard to say, damn it? *I was afraid.*"

My hands itch again with the desire to touch him, to reach for his hand, to slip my arm through his. I don't. "You were?"

"Yes. I do push people away. I have forever. It's usually better that way." He looks away from me, moving restlessly from side to side. "And with you... I'm bound to fuck up in one way or another, Blair. We both know that. It was safer to do it earlier rather than later. Less damage that way."

I bite my lip to hide the hints of a smile. "What if you don't fuck up?"

He shoots me an exasperated look, and I hold up my hands. "All right, all right. Let's say that you will."

"Yeah. And you... being with you would never be just something. It would be everything. You're that kind of woman."

"I—"

"Yes, you are," he says darkly, almost accusingly, and I close my mouth. "You deserve nothing less. And I don't know if I can be conventional. If I can do the parties and the photos and the mingling. But I want to try."

"Try what, exactly?"

"Dating. You and me. *This.*" He extends a hand from me to himself, as if the chemistry between us was a visible thing. I suppose it almost has been, clear from the very beginning. "If you'll have me."

"If I'll have you?" I'm stuck in the incredulity phase. The agitated, passionate Nick in front of me is one I've never seen before.

"Yes, if you'll have me," he repeats. "Despite the fact that it'll mar your public reputation. Damn it, Blair... do you know why I pushed you away for all those years?"

"Self-preservation," I whisper. My body still feels shell-shocked by the words I've wanted to hear from him forever, and here they all are, pouring out like a flash flood, changing the landscape irrevocably.

"It was." Nick steps closer, a large hand reaching up to tip back my head. His dark eyes are soft now, even if tension lingers on his features. "If you'd have been nice to me, if we'd been friends... I wouldn't have been able to stop myself from trying to get closer."

"I would have let you," I murmur.

He closes his eyes, like the words bring him pain. "I suspected as much," he mutters. "Good thing I stayed away."

My hands come up to grip his jacket. "Why?"

"I would have fucked it up," he says, "and far worse than I have this time around."

I reach up on my tiptoes and put my arms around his neck. He leans into my touch, his eyes closing again, our foreheads touching. "I don't think I've ever heard you talk this much in one go," I murmur.

He snorts. "The monologue is over now."

"It was very enlightening."

"Was it?"

"Yes."

"Good. That was the intention."

I slide my hand down to thread my fingers through his and pull him to my couch. He sinks down beside me. "But I don't understand one part."

"Which one?"

I lean back against the pillows and settle my legs over his. His hand reaches out to grip my thigh, like the contact is just as important to the both of us.

"*Why* were you afraid of coming close? Why did pushing me away feel safer?"

He plays with the side-hem of my trousers. "Is this a therapist's couch?"

"It could be," I say, aiming for teasing. "Lean back and let me ask the questions."

His lip curls slightly. "I'm not sure I could handle that."

"You're right. There are too many pillows on this couch. They'd only distract you."

"They definitely would." His fingers trail up my thigh, and even through the fabric, the warmth of his skin sends shivers through me.

I sit up. His hands leave me only for a moment as I rearrange myself on top of him, a leg on either side of his lap. "We communicate much better when we're touching," I say.

His hands settle on my hips. "I've noticed that, too."

"Good thing we have no problem getting physical."

A thumb smooths up my ribcage. "No problem at all."

I run a hand through the shortness of his hair, down over the rough stubble of his jaw. "Will you tell me *something*, at least? Where did you grow up?"

"Oregon," he says. "A tiny town."

"Oh?"

"Nothing to do and not enough money to go around. People were forever unemployed. Houses stood empty. Everyone wanted out and nobody knew how to leave."

I slip my hands inside his jacket and feel the quick beating of his heart. "But you left."

His eyes harden. "I did."

My mind fills in the rest of the story. Traveling north. Loans for college. Befriending Cole. Becoming someone else in Seattle, someone with a penchant for ruthless success.

His hand becomes a fist against my hip. "There was no way I could stay there. And once I'd left, no way I'd let myself fail."

"You haven't," I murmur, wondering if all the tales of Nicholas Park, ruthless venture capitalist, ever get to the heart of the man. That he's doing this for survival and not solely ambition.

"Cole had the same chip on his shoulder." Nick leans his head back against the couch, looking up at me through lidded eyes. "Only his came from his old man and not the memory of crushing poverty."

I swallow hard, keeping my hands on his chest. It's strong and hard under my touch. "Does he know this story?"

"He knows enough of it."

"And what about your family?"

He reaches out and touches my cheek gently, the back of a knuckle sliding over my jaw. "Gone, a long time ago."

There's more there. Of course there is. But we have time, and for now… I lean in and press my lips to his, pouring all my longing for him into that simple touch.

He groans against my lips and his hands come up to rest gently on my shoulder blades. It's a kiss to seal, a kiss to start things. A we-will-have-many-more-of-these kind of kiss.

His words are spoken against my lips. "So you forgive me? For what I said last week?"

I kiss him in reply.

And when he pulls away, hands knotting at my thighs, head bowed against my shoulder, I know what he needs. It's the same thing I ache for.

I tug at his jacket and he obliges, pulling it off and tossing it aside. His hands grip the hem of my shirt and I lift my arms high, letting him pull it off.

His hands burn against my bare skin. "Blair, I…"

"I know."

He lifts me up, held against his body, as we walk toward the bedroom. I don't stop kissing his neck as we do. It's been two weeks since we did this. Two weeks of wondering and indecision and wanting, and now that he's here, now that he's explained…

His grip on my skin is tight. He kisses his way down to my bra and tugs at the cups, mouth settling over my nipples. I close my eyes at the sensations. Warmth races through my veins with each flick of his tongue.

He continues downwards, kissing my stomach, hands on the buttons of my trousers. "I've missed your body so much," he says against my skin. "I've been such an idiot."

A laugh breaks through my haze of lust. "We both have."

"No, not you. Never you." He pulls my trousers off and then he's back, kissing my lips, and I wrap my arms around him. He's hard against me. "Blair, I want to try."

I hitch my leg around his hip. "I think you can do more than just try."

He breaks away from my lips to laugh darkly. "I meant with us."

"Oh."

"If I fuck up again… don't hate me."

"I won't." I reach up and grip his face, a hand on either side. "*If* you take me down off whatever pedestal you have me on."

His eyes narrow. "Blair—"

"I mean it. I'm certainly not flawless. I choose this, too. I choose you."

He rolls his hips once, pushing against me, and my breath comes out in a small gasp. "Say that again."

"I choose you?"

"Yeah."

Laughing, I run my hands up his broad back, marveling at the feel of his muscles underneath his warm skin. "I choose you," I say. "I choose you, I choose you—"

And then he's kissing me again, and there isn't much thought left. Underwear is discarded and his hands, despite the roughness of the scarred palms, are soft on my skin.

"Yes," he tells me when I open my mouth.

"I wasn't going to protest."

He settles between my thighs. "Sure you weren't."

But I wasn't. No, when his tongue begins its sensual assault, I relax entirely into the sensations. Want and lust and heat and beneath it all, joy. That he's here. That we've talked. That there is suddenly an *us*, even if it's a new and fragile thing.

His hands grip my hips to keep me from arching away from him as I shatter. He grins as he rises up between my legs.

"I knew you'd eventually grow to love that."

"You were right."

"Don't think it'll ever stop satisfying me."

"Me neither," I say, and I'm rewarded by his dark laughter.

He positions himself and then he's inside and there is no more talk. It's just this joining and our breath and the feel of his body against mine, warm and large.

Afterwards, he stretches out beside me and tucks me against his body. I rest my head against his shoulder and focus on calming my breathing. Beneath me, his heart is beating fast.

"You know what they'll say," Nick says, his hand sweeping up my back.

"What?"

"About us. About you and me."

For a moment, I wonder if I can feign ignorance. But then I nod. "Perhaps a few of the gossip columns will. For about a week, until someone decides to get a very public divorce or a celebrity sex tape leaks."

Nick's voice rumbles through his chest. "People will keep thinking it long after that. The narrative is as old as time. Seattle's darling socialite and the most despised investor on this side of the country."

"I don't care."

His arms tighten around me, but there's skepticism in his silence. I rise up on my elbow and meet his gaze. "I genuinely don't. What do they know, anyway? About you, about me, about us?"

"Nothing."

"Exactly. Now, do I have to go get a decorative pillow so you can punch out your fears?"

His face breaks into a wide smile. "I'd destroy the pillow."

"That's all right. I have a hundred more."

"So you don't mind? Truly? I thought you might, considering your strong reaction to all those critics last time."

"No, I don't." I lean in, rubbing my nose against his. It's a silly gesture, but it provokes another one of his rare smiles. "Let them talk."

"Your skin has gotten thicker."

"I'm less afraid," I say. "Someone taught me that."

He leans back and puts an arm behind his head, the one not holding me. "Funny. Someone taught me that, too."

For a moment, we just smile at each other.

"There's just one more thing," I say.

"Oh?"

"What are we going to tell Cole? We can't have you two avoiding each other indefinitely."

Nick's smile turns crooked. "Well, about that…"

"Yeah?"

"I think he'll come around."

I narrow my eyes at him. "So you two have spoken?"

"Briefly. He made it clear that I should have chosen someone else for my… affections, but having made the choice I did, I'd better fix things. 'Make my sister happy,' I believe he said."

I roll my eyes. "Thank God he *told* you to do that."

"Yes, it was very helpful," Nick says. "I would never have thought of that on my own."

And then I'm smiling as I kiss him, and he's kissing me back, the ball of happiness in my chest near bursting.

25

NICK

A few weeks later

"Are you really *sure*?"

I roll my eyes at the question. It's not the first time she's asked today. "Yes, of course I'm sure."

Blair slips her arm under mine. "Well, if it gets too much…"

"I'm not that weak." I lean down, pushing her hair back so I can whisper in her ear. "If anything, you're the one who should be nervous."

"I should?"

"Nobody will dare ask *me* about our relationship. You'll be the one fending off questions."

Her smile falters, but then her eyes flare with triumph. The hand on my arm digs in. "I won't let you leave my side, then."

"Think you can stop me?"

"Oh, I've been practicing," she warns. Yes, that she has indeed. Curious as ever, Blair has joined my sessions with my kickboxing trainer twice a week. At first, I'd agreed just to humor her, but seeing her with braided hair, determination in her eyes, sweat glistening on her skin… yeah. It had been a good idea.

"That you have."

"Wait," she says, reaching up to fix the lapels of my jacket. I can't resist. "Are you stalling?"

"No," she says, but her lips quirk at the corners. "I'm just making sure we make the best possible entrance."

Looking down at her dress, at the matching pocket square in my suit jacket… she's already gone all out. "Come on, coward," I say, pushing the front door open. "After you."

We step into Winter Wonderland. Gone is Cole and Skye's tastefully decorated foyer. A giant Christmas tree is front and center, an assortment of silver baubles evenly spaced. The staircase is fringed with winter-green garlands. In the air, the scent of cinnamon and mulled wine hangs heavily.

"Oh," Blair breathes. "It's *beautiful.*"

It is. The warm Christmas lighting is giving her blonde hair, loose around her face, an almost luminous sheen. "Yes."

An attendant takes our jackets as a singer begins to softly croon *"All I Want for Christmas"* from the built-in stereo system. I wonder who Cole's invited this time. You never know who you'll encounter at an event where he's had a hand on the invites.

Blair's fingers thread through mine. The gesture comes naturally to her now, as does throwing an arm around my shoulders while I'm working, or sitting down on my lap instead of a free chair. The easy, trusting way she touches me never fails to strike me.

"Let's go say hello," she says.

We head into the living room. There's a smaller Christmas tree here in the corner, but this one looks decidedly more homey. None of the baubles match. Definitely the work of Skye and Timmy and not any party decorators.

One after one, the gathered guests begin to notice us. First Blair. Then me. And finally our joined hands.

It's almost comical, the surprise in their eyes when they piece it together. While most of the people here know Blair quite well, very, very few know me at all.

Yes, this had been an excellent place for this.

Blair pulls me along to say hello to her cousin. Hugs ensue, and I shake a few hands, introducing myself to people I *might* have met before but have forgotten, either way.

Blair's cousin gives her a very unsubtle glance, eyes briefly flicking back to me. The message is clear. *You two? Why haven't you told me?*

I smile. Yes, Blair will practically be drowned in questions after this. I look forward to hearing a few of her replies for myself.

Cole finds me a while later, leaning against one of the walls. Silently, he hands me a glass of brandy. "Thought you might need something a bit stronger."

"I'm not about to bolt."

"Just in case," he says, his grin wolfish. "So you two chose to upstage my Christmas party, huh?"

"It was Blair's idea. I don't really care where we 'come out,' as she so tactfully phrased it, but she thought this was the best place for it."

Strike, likely bewildered by all the people, weaves through legs to come sit at Cole's feet. His tongue lolls out of his mouth, paws too big for his body. "Hi, buddy," Cole says. "Yes, well, perhaps she was right about that."

I take a sip of my brandy. It's far more grounding than the champagne I had earlier; Cole knows me well. "Is it still weird?"

He raises an eyebrow. "You dating my sister?"

"Yes. And if so, at what point does it *stop* being weird to you, do you think?" I'm pushing it, perhaps. He's been very good these past few weeks, never once mentioning anything about Blair and me in front of her. The four of us have even been out to dinner together—all of *one* time. It's been grating on Blair. In her mind, I think she always envisioned this as a seamless thing.

Cole leans on the wall beside me. "I don't know," he says. "I know you independently, and I know her independently, and seeing you together… I just don't know."

I nod. It's not unexpected, but it still stings a little bit, especially knowing that I'm not who he would have chosen for his sister.

So I can't resist. "You used to say that you wanted us to get along better."

He shoots me a withering glare and I hold up my hands in apology. "I couldn't help myself. As long as I don't get my godparent-to-be status revoked."

Shaking his head, he swirls his whiskey around in his glass. "It's not revoked. And if you want my honest opinion... I'm cautiously optimistic. She's glowing with happiness, you know. And she's more determined than ever with her work. I do think you have a little bit to do with that. And you're... well, Nick, you don't scowl quite as much."

Selfish, vain pride courses through me at the *glowing with happiness* comment. "Right."

"But I'll be right here to tell you off if you fuck up."

"I wouldn't have it any other way."

"And if it's still going well in a few months' time, I'll consider letting the two of you stay in the chalet."

I chuckle. "How magnanimous of you."

"Skye keeps telling me the signs were all there. *I knew before they knew,* she says, like she'll get some sort of medal." He snorts. "Worst part is, perhaps she's right."

"She might be. She's intuitive, your wife."

Cole nods. "Perhaps I was just blind. If I hadn't been so *sure* you two disliked each other, so sure that you were complete opposites, I wouldn't have been so surprised."

"She surprised me too," I say.

"And the more I think about it, the more sense the two of you make." He shakes his head again, but this time, there's a small smile on his face. "To think I might one day call you brother-in-law."

"Imagine that," I say. His voice hadn't sounded entirely displeased, either.

"And you're not cringing from that statement, either? Christ. The world really has turned upside down."

"It has. You're a father in, what, four months?"

"Four months, two weeks, and six days."

"Not counting at all, are you?"

He takes another sip of his whiskey, his eyes focused on Skye now. The burgundy dress fits snugly around her baby bump. "I'm a shameless counter," he says, voice far away. "I even have one of those apps that lets me follow along."

I shake my head at him, but it's good-natured, and when my eyes land on Blair again... She really is glowing. Talking to Skye, her arms gesturing as she discusses some topic. It's easy for my mind to imagine her round with child, instead. My child.

Dear God.

"We really are whipped," I note.

Cole snorts beside me. "Gladly."

Ethan finds us like that. He's become a staple on Cole's guest lists and an increasingly common tennis opponent. I've found that I don't mind at all. The man has a decent backhand and an indecent sense of humor. Too bad he's a single dad with basically no time for playing.

With a brandy glass of his own, he nods at the guests. "I've said it before, but you throw excellent parties, Porter."

Cole tears his gaze away from his wife to nod at Ethan. "You should try it sometime. We're practically neighbors, and yet I've never been to yours. At this point it's practically an insult."

Ethan's smile is crooked. "Yes, well, I have two little hooligans at home who have black belts in wreaking havoc."

"I'll have one soon, too," Cole points out.

"Yes, but I hate to break it to you, they don't do much for the first year."

"Oh?"

"They really only graduate to hooligan level after the year and a half mark," Ethan says.

"And what are they when they're teenagers?" I ask dryly.

Ethan pretends to shudder. "I have no idea yet, thankfully. Terrorist, perhaps? I should begin to prepare."

"Build a safe room under your house," Cole suggests. "Surely Greenwood zoning regulations allow that?"

I slip away quietly from the discussion of paternal struggles to find Blair. She's no longer talking to Skye or her mother, but rather engaged in an animated discussion with a few of her friends. I recognize them instantly.

This should be good.

Coming up behind her, I revel in their wide-eyed gazes as I wrap an arm around her waist. Touching her grounds me—there's no other way to describe it.

She looks up at me with warm, golden-brown eyes. "Hey."

"Hi. What are we talking about?"

The friend across from her—I think her name is Maddie—gives me a hesitant smile. I vaguely remember her from a wedding months ago. Her smile had been flirty then. "Well, we were discussing... the candied apples. They're served in the dining room. Have you had one yet?"

"No," I say seriously. "I haven't."

Two of the men standing by her side shuffle from side to side, a tad uneasy.

"Come," Blair tells me. "Let me show you."

She pulls me into the considerably less crowded dining room. "Oh my God, thank you for getting me out of there."

"Anytime." Reaching up, I run a tendril of her golden hair through my fingers. "What exactly was I saving you from? I thought you liked your friends."

"You used to call them a posse," she teases. "A clique."

"Yes, because they love you for your attention. And perhaps because I was jealous."

Her smile stretches wider. "We were talking about you. They couldn't believe I'd kept it a secret. They couldn't really believe it at all, actually."

"They'll likely tell everyone."

"Most probably," she says. "Maddie can't keep a secret to save her life."

There's no trace of resignation on her face—only a teasing

smile and glittering eyes. "Well, I have to say, calling you mine in public has a nice ring to it," I say.

"You think?"

"Yes." And then, not caring who's in the room or who's watching, I bend down to press my lips to hers. She kisses me back, arms circling my neck, sweeter than any Christmas candy. Funny how this never gets old, having her lips to explore and her warm mouth opening for me.

She sighs softly against me. "You know, I really love you," she murmurs.

The words are like a detonation. They bounce around in my head, my mind as resistant to them as a damn Teflon pan in a TV advert, refusing to stick.

She can't love me. Not possibly. Not really.

Blair draws back with a smile. "Knew you'd react like that," she teases. "So I'll give you a week or two to think about them before I'll say it again."

I capture her lips with mine again. She loves me. And she's not the least bit concerned about saying it, about me reciprocating, or worried about what this will mean.

If she's brave enough to say the words, then I'm brave enough to accept them.

She finally pulls away, her cheeks beautifully flushed. "We *are* still at a party," she murmurs. "I didn't expect that, well, *that* would be your response."

I tuck her into my side. She loves me. I'll have to repeat it to myself over and over again until it becomes real. "Blair, I…"

"I know," she says, putting a hand over my heart. "I know. We have time."

Those might be the most beautiful words I've ever heard.

EPILOGUE

BLAIR

"A whole weekend without work," I say. "I'm still not sure if I can do it."

There's a smile in Nick's voice when he replies. "Yes, you can."

"But what if there's an emergency? A server crashes, or an order form gets mixed up, or a newspaper urgently needs an interview?"

"Your assistant knows to call you if there's an emergency," he says. It's not the first time he's reassured me like this. "And CEOs get to take vacations."

"Neither you nor Cole took one for your first five years in business."

He puts down the suitcase and shuts the front door to the chalet with his foot. "Be smarter than us," he tells me. "Just be here with me for a few days."

He's right. I reach up and press a kiss to his cheek, forcing away thoughts of orders and packaging and overhead. "I'm sorry. For the coming few days, I'll be yours entirely, body, soul and mind."

"I thought you always were."

Sticking out my tongue at him, I walk through the beautiful space. Outside the floor-to-ceiling windows, the snow is falling softly. It's early March and prime season in Whistler. "Hot tub right away?"

Nick chuckles. "Did you just read my mind?"

"Maybe. I've been practicing."

As we get dressed and settled, my mind wanders back to the company by its own accord. The launch was just a month ago—and it's been nonstop work since then.

And to my surprise… it's doing really well.

The newspapers I'd spoken to were interested in full-page interviews and that really got the word out. And the young marketing expert I'd hired—straight out of college, no less—was amazing. Ingenious, even. She'd once commented that my relationship with Nick was *helping* my brand.

He'd had a field day with that comment.

Smiling, I look over at Nick. He's tugging off his cable-knit sweater on the other side of the master bedroom. He'd been there for the launch party, of course.

And he'd been far tougher than I'd been. "The banner is crooked," he'd pointed out.

"It is?"

"Yes. And something is off with the lighting."

I'd caught his arm. "Don't worry about it."

"It's not good enough." He'd shrugged off my hands casually. "I'll fix it. You should have the best."

And he had. In the midst of the preparations he'd been there, barking orders right alongside me in the way that only he could.

And the launch party was better for it.

"Why are you looking at me like that?" he asks, pulling on his trunks.

My smile widens. "I don't know. I think I just kinda like you."

He smiles at that, too. Funny, how much more often he does that these days. "Flatterer," he says.

"And I'm thinking that you must have enjoyed the email from the Adams, even if you refuse to admit it."

He rolls his eyes. "Their approval doesn't matter."

"I'm not saying it does," I say. At the same time, though, the fact that they had finally come around to seeing merit in what Nick had done—that B.C. Adams now has seventy stores operating nationwide and beginning to turn a tentative profit... "But it doesn't hurt. And saving a company must be a fun change of pace."

He reaches for me, pulling me into his side as we walk down the hallway. "Fine—it was a nice email. Don't get your hopes up, though. I'm already looking for another company to butcher."

I snort. "I wouldn't have you any other way."

We uncover the hot tub, steam rising into the cold, freezing air. Snowdrifts frame the cleared patio, close enough to reach out and touch.

Smiling angelically at Nick, I form a snowball.

"No," he says. "Absolutely not."

"You wanted me to relax."

"Relax, not fight." He climbs into the hot tub, the width of his shoulders rising out of the hot water. "If you're itching for it, I can bring up our living situation again."

I drop the snowball and glare at him. He chuckles, not bothered in the least by my death look. His laughter comes much more freely now.

"Fine, I won't," he says. "Now will you please get in here? It's killing me to see you in a bikini from so far away. I need access."

Rolling my eyes at that, I climb into the hot tub after him. "My apartment has everything I need," I can't resist saying. "My assistant has the space she needs, too. It's like a little headquarters."

"So make it into that."

He's not joking. "You think?"

"Yes. Turn it into your office and move in with me instead."

Slicing through the water, I cover the short distance to him and into his waiting arms. "Into your apartment?"

"No," he says, tucking me against his large form. "It has

209

absolutely no charm, as you've pointed out enough times. No decorative pillows though, but that's really the only plus."

I elbow him and he rolls his eyes, the picture of reluctance. "Fine, fine. You'll be allowed a few in our new place. Choose wisely where you'll put them. Couch or bed, but you can't have both."

"You're cruel."

He presses a kiss to my temple. "I don't care where we live, Blair. Just as long as you're sleeping in my bed every night."

I relax into the warm water and his embrace. "Well, I know I said I was dead-set against it…"

"Yes?"

"But there *is* a place in Cole and Skye's area for sale. I know it's too soon for us. But it did get me thinking… perhaps Greenwood Hills wouldn't be so bad?"

Nick snorts. "So you want us to do the whole thing? White-picket fence and a dog and a baby on the way."

"No dog," I say. "And no baby. Not yet, anyway. And the fence doesn't even have to be white. There are a ton of other possible colors, a whole rainbow of them. I'm open to suggestions."

His hand toys with the side-knot of my bikini bottoms. "I doubt the neighborhood association would allow for a rainbow fence," he says. "But like I said, I don't care much where we live. And being close to Cole and Skye… well, I know it would make you happy."

"Not to mention it'll make *you* happy, too," I point out. "No point in denying it."

He grumbles in response, but I know it's the truth. Nick and Cole are thick as thieves again, though it had taken a few months for the both of them to adjust to the new dynamic.

My brother had even winked when he told us to take the chalet this weekend. "Don't tear the place down completely," he'd said. I wasn't sure what I felt about *that* type of joke, but he was on board, and that's what mattered.

"Remember when we were up here last time, watching those glaciers and ice caves?" I ask.

"Of course I do."

"They were gorgeous. Beyond anything I've seen. And still... I just kept thinking about how you'd seen me as a grown woman for the first time the night before. It was the first time I'd ever really felt hopeful where you were concerned."

His voice drops an octave, the huskiness in it settling in my stomach. "Believe me, I have never seen you as anything else. That was the whole problem."

"Even from the beginning?"

His hands grip my waist, lifting me onto his lap. Our bodies fit easily together in the warm water. "Even from the beginning."

"I know that means you were basically pining for years, just like me, which isn't nice... but it selfishly makes me a bit happy to hear, too."

His smile is crooked, a wet hand reaching up to cup my cheek. "Of course it does."

Our kiss is sweet. They're increasingly common, these soft kisses—ones that speak of a future. Not rushed and filled with instantaneous passion, although there's often plenty of that, too.

"There are no neighbors around, right?"

Nick's eyes are heated as he looks from me to the wide expanse of snow-covered firs. "No. An errant squirrel, perhaps. A moose."

"They can watch." I untie my bikini top, loving the way his eyes darken.

His hands replace the dark fabric and our kisses turn from sweet to heated. He presses his face to my neck, lips on my skin. "I love you."

Funny, how those words never stop affecting me, not when they're spoken in his gravelly voice. Especially not when his scarred hands are on my skin, and when it's just the two of us and a lifetime of togetherness to look forward to. He'd said it about a month after I did, and when he did... it was well worth the wait.

"I love you too," I say, gasping as he undoes the knots of my bikini bottoms and pulls them out of the way.

"That was smart," he comments. "Can't all your panties be like that?"

"I'll consider it for the next collection." My voice is breathless, hands gripping his shoulders as his fingers begin to move between my legs.

"One more thing," he says.

"What?"

"We'll live wherever you want. Hell, fill the place with decorative pillows to your heart's content. But I want a small ceremony, Blair. I know how you Porters like it big."

I roll my hips against him to emphasize those words and we both laugh for a moment, the husky sounds mingling in the cold air.

Then his words break through my haze of desire. "The *ceremony*?" Had I really heard that word from his lips?

"I will ask you one day, you know." His voice is teasing, but his dark, heated eyes are serious.

I rest my forehead against his. "Wow," I murmur, doing my best to hold on to this man, to the sensations he's making me feel, emotional and physical all at the same time.

"Nothing else to say? That's not like you."

"Hinting at marriage? That's not like you, either," I echo.

He laughs, hands moving quicker now. Perhaps this was what he wanted to say. "I've decided something," he says. "Well, I decided it weeks ago."

"Oh? And what was that?"

"If I'm going to do this, I'm going to do it right, Blair. I'm all in. So no more tip-toeing around me when you suggest couple's dinners. No more sly hints about wanting to go to Oregon and see my hometown."

I grimace. "Not so sly after all?"

"You're the sneakiest," he assures me. "But there's no need. I'm not about to bolt. Not now, and not later."

"Good. Because you know I wouldn't let you," I say, my

words breaking into a gasp when his fingers circle a particularly sensitive spot. "There's no place you could go where I wouldn't find you and try to drag you out. Not even your own melancholy."

Nick presses his lips against mine. "And I'll be your punching bag, whenever you need one."

My laughing reply is cut off entirely as he moves, as his fingers circle, forcing me to tighten my grip on his shoulders. And there's no fear at all in this surrender, not from him and not from me, with only the wide-open sky as our witness and the falling snow as our companion.

AFTERWORD

The Seattle Billionaires series isn't over yet!

Ethan Carter's story is coming in November of 2020, and it's a delicious single dad, billionaire age gap romance.

ABOUT OLIVIA

Olivia loves billionaire heroes despite never having met one in person. Taking matters into her own hands, she creates them on the page instead. Stern, charming, cold or brooding, so far she's never met a (fictional) billionaire she didn't like.

A voracious reader of romance, Olivia picked up the pen a few years back and what followed was nothing short of a love affair of her own. Now she spends her days giggling at the steamy banter she's writing or swooning at their happily-ever-afters.

Smart and sexy romance—those are her lead themes!

Join her newsletter at www.oliviahayle.com for bonus content.

Connect with Olivia

facebook.com/authoroliviahayle
instagram.com/oliviahayle
goodreads.com/oliviahayle
amazon.com/author/oliviahayle
bookbub.com/profile/olivia-hayle

Printed in Great Britain
by Amazon